PLANNING THE WEDDING

- ❏ Families meet
  (get mother-in-law's approval)
- ❏ Choose church
  (mother-in-law's choice)
- ❏ Decide on guest list
  (mother-in-law's decision)
- ❏ Select wedding gown
  (mother-in-law's selection)
- ❏ Pick attendants
  (mother-in-law's choice)
- ❏ Select bridesmaids' dresses
  (rely on mother-in-law's good taste)
- ❏ Write wedding vows
  (bride will obey)
- ❏ Select music for ceremony
  (mother-in-law's selections)
- ❏ Choose place for reception
  (mother-in-law's choice)
- ❏ Select music for reception
  (mother-in-law's favorites)
- ❏ Plan seating arrangement
  (mother-in-law knows best)
- ❏ Arrange for video and photographs
  (mother-in-law will choose and assist)
- ❏ Menu plan
  (mother-in-law's plan)
- ❏ Honeymoon
  (take mother-in-law along?)

Avon Books are available at special quantity discounts for bulk purchases for sales promotions, premiums, fund raising or educational use. Special books, or book excerpts, can also be created to fit specific needs.

For details write or telephone the office of the Director of Special Markets, Avon Books, Dept. FP, 1350 Avenue of the Americas, New York, New York 10019, 1-800-238-0658.

Brides

Heather's Change of Heart

ZÖE COOPER

AN AVON FLARE BOOK

AVON BOOKS
A division of
The Hearst Corporation
1350 Avenue of the Americas
New York, New York 10019

Copyright © 1997 by By George Productions, Inc.
Published by arrangement with the author
Visit our website at **http://AvonBooks.com**
Library of Congress Catalog Card Number: 97-93769
ISBN: 0-380-78701-6
RL: 5.9

First Avon Flare Printing: December 1997

AVON FLARE TRADEMARK REG. U.S. PAT. OFF. AND IN OTHER COUNTRIES,
MARCA REGISTRADA, HECHO EN U.S.A.

Printed in the U.S.A.

WCD   10 9 8 7 6 5 4 3 2 1

For Ronda Brown,
who understands the three things that matter:
Faith, Hope, and Love

The treehouse seemed much smaller. Of course, the last time she'd climbed into it, she'd been about ten. Now Heather Johnson was thirteen, and her slender brown legs were almost as long as the rest of her.

Heather tilted her head back and squinted at the wooden structure. The nailed-together old boards looked awfully flimsy. Maybe this idea wasn't so great after all.

Suddenly, a head popped out of the opening. "What are you waiting for? An engraved invitation?" Sherri Deiter called. Her long red braid swung like a pendulum as she grinned down at Heather.

Another head popped out next to Sherri's. Corinne Janowski's sea-green eyes were sad, but she tried to smile. "Or are you just a scaredy-cat?" she teased.

"One more word and you die," Heather called. She grabbed for the first low branch.

Her hands and feet found the familiar knots and bumps of the tree as if she'd just climbed it yesterday. Heather scrambled up the trunk easily. Her head rose through the opening, and she squeezed into the treehouse.

It was a tight fit. Heather sat down next to Corinne. Now that she was close up, she could see that Corinne had been crying.

It had been Sherri's wacky inspiration to meet in their

old clubhouse. Now Heather knew how right Sherri was. On this sad day, they needed to return to the place where their friendship had begun. The treehouse was where they'd formed their secret club in first grade, when they'd met and become best friends.

But today, their threesome was breaking up. Corinne's parents were getting a divorce, and Corinne was moving north to Berkeley.

"I can't believe how many hours we spent in this place," Corinne said, gently touching the worn wood. "And I can't believe I have to leave you guys." Her eyes filled with tears. "Let's face it, my life is over."

"No, it isn't," Heather said sternly. She was afraid that if she let herself, she'd burst into tears. Then Corinne would *really* start to cry, and Sherri would join in, and they'd all just feel worse.

"It just feels that way," she continued soothingly to Corinne. "At least you're in the same *state*. San Francisco is a totally fun place to visit. We'll come on vacations, and in the meantime, we'll write."

"I'll call," Sherri corrected with a grin. "You know how hopeless I am at writing letters. But I can stay on the phone for hours. Just ask my dad."

"Nothing can take away from our friendship," Heather said firmly. "We're friends forever, remember?"

She held out her hand, palm down. Sherri placed her slender hand on top of it. After a pause, Corinne put her own hand on top of Sherri's.

"Friends forever," they said together. "Through thick and thin."

Heather looked down at the stack of hands. As always, she noted how brown her hand was next to her best friends'. Some of her black friends thought it was weird that she was so close to two white girls.

But the way Heather looked at it, she'd had no choice. From the day she'd beaten the bully Donny Canarsie in a foot race in first grade, Corinne and Sherri had singled her out for friendship. They'd liked all the same things. Thought the same things were funny. Thought the same things were gross. The Three Musketeers, everyone called them.

Because her parents were active in the community and belonged to a Baptist church, she never lacked for African-American friends. But most of her time was spent with Sherri and Corinne. Heather had long ago stopped worrying about whether it looked strange or not.

A tear dripped onto Corinne's hand. She'd started to cry again. Heather's own eyes filled with tears. She'd miss Corinne so much! Sherri was the wild one. She was unpredictable, funny, and occasionally bossy. Corinne's sweetness and kind heart was a good balance. She was the one who could puncture Sherri's balloon and make her come down to earth. She usually did it with a quiet joke, and Sherri was usually the one to laugh hardest of all. And Corinne was the one to make Heather lighten up when she got too focused on success in school and athletics and forgot to have fun.

"Don't worry, Corinne," Sherri said miserably. "Heather is right. We'll be friends forever. Till we're old and married."

Suddenly, a fierce gleam lit Corinne's green eyes. "I'm never getting married," she declared. "Look what happens. You just break up."

"Not always," Heather pointed out. "Sherri's parents are still together. And mine are practically Siamese twins. It's just bad luck, Corinne. You'll be smarter than your parents. You'll find the perfect guy."

"I'm going to live alone with lots of animals," Corinne said, shaking her head so that her honey-brown hair brushed her cheeks. "I'm never getting married."

Heather tucked her long brown legs underneath her chin and traded a worried glance with Sherri. "I'll make you a deal," she proposed. "I'll get married first to test it out. If I think the deal is okay, I'll let you guys know."

"How do you know we'll still be friends?" Corinne

asked gloomily. She picked at a sliver of wood. "That's years and years and years away. Look how everything changes."

Suddenly, Sherri sat up straight. "I've got it! We'll have a pact. We'll all be each other's bridesmaids at our weddings. No matter where we are, or who we marry."

"No matter what," Heather agreed.

Sherri giggled. "Even if I marry a guy with a wart on his nose in Timbuktu, you guys have to come."

To Heather's relief, Corinne started to smile. Leave it to Sherri to lighten the atmosphere.

"Heather will probably marry some rich, handsome, perfect guy," Corinne teased, twisting a strand of hair around one finger. "She does everything right."

"Heather's perfect," Sherri agreed, waving a hand.

Heather felt color sting her cheeks. "I'm not," she mumbled. "I just try hard, that's all."

Heather's parents were schoolteachers. *Education* and *achievement* weren't just words in the Johnson household. Her older brothers were both going to Ivy League colleges. And her sister Talia, a junior in high school, kept up a solid A average, as well as being editor of the school paper. Sometimes, all that "achievement" could be hard to live up to.

Sherri rode over Heather's words. She waved her hands excitedly in the air. "I know just how my wedding will be. On a beach. I'll wear a white dress with a six-foot train. And purple taffeta dresses for the bridesmaids."

"You won't catch me in purple taffeta," Heather said, shaking her head. "But I *am* going to wear red at my wedding."

"Red?" Sherri hooted. "And you call *me* crazy!"

"I like red," Heather said.

"Maybe because Greg Tolliver likes that red sweater of yours," Corinne teased. She put a finger on her chin, pretending to be puzzled. "And aren't basketball forwards supposed to be great fashion consultants?"

Sherri laughed. "Well, if you marry Greg, you can wear red," she told Heather.

"Marry Greg?" Heather shuddered. "No way. My husband isn't going to be a stringbean goofball. He's got to be tall, because I am. But he's got to be smart, and ambitious, and funny, and most of all, he's got to be a good dancer. And a good cook," she added. "Because I'm not going to cook. No way."

"Um, and does he have to have won the Nobel Prize?" Corinne teased.

"Or have climbed Mount Everest?" Sherri giggled.

"Naturally," Heather said with a grin.

"A perfect husband for a perfect wife equals the perfect life," Corinne said with an exaggerated sigh. Sherri hooted with laughter, and Heather laughed, too.

But Heather didn't want to be a perfect person. She just wanted to be . . . herself.

One

Nine years later

Heather stared at the misshapen dough on the kitchen counter. She sighed. "Just tell me this. Does it at least *resemble* a pizza?"

Her roommate, Jake Deveraux, squinted at it behind his wire-rimmed glasses. "It looks like a traffic accident."

Heather giggled. "At least I have a doctor handy," she said to him.

Jake, a medical student, grinned at her. "We could bring it to the E.R.," he suggested.

She groaned. "They have enough to do. Well, I have great hopes for the one in the oven. In the meantime, let's make a total veggie pizza." She reached for the knife and began slicing broccoli.

So far, her pizza making had turned out a string of failures. But Heather really didn't mind. The soft Atlanta spring breeze wafted through the kitchen window, stirring a curl by her ear. It brought the scent of magnolias and sunshine into the kitchen.

Over the past two years, it had been rare for Heather to have an entire day off. In graduate school for her master's in social work, she was in an accelerated program, and juggled a heavy class schedule. Not to mention that she spent long hours at the hospital for her internship.

"Uh, Heather?" Jake asked. "Have you checked the oven lately?"

"No," she answered. "Why?"

"Because there's smoke coming out," Jake said.

With a cry, Heather ran to the oven door and banged it open. "Shoot!" she exclaimed, reaching for the pizza.

"Heather!" Jake barked. "Don't—"

But it was too late. Heather burned her fingers as she grabbed for the pan. "Owwww!" she yelled, backing up.

Jake moved as fast as lightning. First, he grabbed a potholder and withdrew the smoking pizza pan. Then he swiftly brought Heather to the sink and ran cold water on her hand.

Heather winced. "It's not bad. I barely touched it."

"I'm the doctor," Jake said sternly. "I'll make the diagnosis."

He peered at her fingers. "Hmmm. It's not bad."

Laughing, Heather gave him a swat with her good hand. "I hope I don't owe you a fee for that."

"Keep your hand under the water," Jake chided, smiling. His long, strong fingers circled her wrist gently as he held her hand in the cool stream.

Heather sighed as she gazed at the blackened pizza. "I thought that one would be perfect."

"We'll try again," Jake said. His amber eyes glinted behind his glasses. "I'm in this for the long haul, sister."

With a flick of his wrist, Jake turned off the water. Still holding Heather's arm, he brought her to the cabinet, where he withdrew a small first-aid kit.

"I don't need—"

"Stand still," Jake ordered. His gaze was intent as he concentrated on her reddened finger. Heather stood obediently as he expertly applied a soothing cream and then bandaged the spot.

"You're going to make a great doctor, Jake," she said softly.

His grin was immediate. "Good. Because I make a lousy cook."

Heather giggled. "Just make sure your patients don't see you in that outfit."

Jake looked down at himself. He was wearing jeans and an old sweatshirt, and he was spattered with bright red tomato sauce. He laughed along with her.

"Come on," he said. "Let's get started on that next pie. Just let *me* slice the broccoli."

Smiling, Heather stirred the tomato sauce on the stove. When she had decided to make pizza today, she'd never expected to wind up in the kitchen with Jake. Getting him to take his nose out of his books was an impossible task. But they'd spent a comfortable, joking afternoon together. Even watching dough rise was fun with Jake around.

"Broccoli is chopped. Cheese is shredded. What next?" Jake asked. "I await orders."

"Bring the dough over here, and I'll put sauce on it," Heather said. "Then we'll add the vegetables and cheese. And so help me, if you sneak an anchovy on this one, you're dead meat."

"Don't you mean dead fish?" Jake grinned as he brought the dough over to the stove.

The funny thing was, she'd had a major crush on Jake when they'd met two years before. She'd walked on air when the handsome young med student at the hospital asked her out.

But after only a few dates, Jake gently told her that he couldn't see her any longer. He wasn't ready to get serious; he was completely focused on his work, and it wouldn't be fair to a girl to start a relationship. He would, however, like to be good friends.

Heather had to admit that her pride had been hurt a little bit. But she liked Jake too much to bid him good-bye. She understood him too well. He had a drive to succeed, and he wouldn't let anything threaten that. Jake had grown up in the Chicago projects, and he was determined to succeed for the sake of his hardworking mother and younger brother. His dedication had paid off. Academically, he was at the top of his class, and he was already known as a brilliant diagnostician at the hospital.

They'd been able to segue into an easy friendship. Jake alternately teased and ignored her, just like her older brothers. He even called her "Peanut," although she was almost as tall as he was. It had been so easy, in fact, that Heather hadn't hesitated when she'd needed a third roommate. She knew Jake was looking for an apartment, and she'd asked him if he'd like to move in with her and her roommate, Deborah Witkin.

It had been the perfect arrangement. All three of them were in the health care field and shared the same crazy hours. Deborah was studying radiology, and her schedule was just as rough as Heather's and Jake's.

The three of them had spent a hard year, working and studying. They exchanged sleepy smiles in the hallway at six A.M., left each other notes and thermoses of fresh coffee, and constantly ran out of milk and orange juice.

Now the long year was over. Heather was done. Her last paper was written, and she was graduating the very next week. She would be staying on at her internship at the hospital for a few weeks. A patient advocate who helped patients deal with the maze of city services, Heather was hoping her internship would turn into a paying position.

Deborah had packed up and moved back to Florida and her fiancé. Jake would be leaving in August to start his residency at Johns Hopkins in Baltimore. Heather would have to look for new roommates or a smaller apartment, but she wasn't worrying about that yet.

Heather slid the vegetable pie into the oven. "There," she said, dusting flour off her hands. "At last, I have a pie worthy of Reggie Tyler."

"Is it gold-plated?" Jake asked.

"It *should* be," Heather said with a grin. "Only the best for Reggie."

Things worked out as they were meant to, Heather thought, setting the timer. Because Jake had been the one to introduce her to the man of her dreams.

Jake was handsome, but Reggie Tyler had the kind of movie-star looks that made girls swoon. Heather had been no exception. Still, it was Reggie's personality that had won her heart. For Reggie she could find time in her busy schedule. He was so exciting! He was always ready to sweep her off to do something wonderful: dancing at a new club, or a midnight dip in his apartment complex pool. He sent her roses and always called when he said he would. He was the perfect boyfriend. It hadn't taken her long to realize that she was head over heels in love with him.

The timer buzzed, and Heather slipped on an oven mitt and opened the oven door. Reggie did so much for her that she loved thinking of ways to please him. When he'd told her that morning that he was craving pizza for their video date night, she'd decided to make him a homemade pie.

She'd just never dreamed she'd be so *bad* at it.

Jake peered at the pizza. "Looking good, Peanut."

"Really?" Heather asked dubiously. "It looks kind of . . . lopsided to me."

Jake stood back and regarded it. "It does have a certain amoeba-like quality."

They looked at each other and burst out laughing.

"I have a little dough left," Jake said. "Let's try one more."

"Bring it on over," Heather said by the stove. "I have just enough sauce."

Jake headed toward her, balancing the last of the dough on his fists. But he skidded on a pool of spilled water. Heather reached out to steady him and dropped the sauce spoon into the pan, spattering sauce all over her shirt and the stove. The dough flew out of Jake's hands. They both grabbed for it at the same time, pulling it in two. Half of the dough fell into the puddle, and

Heather and Jake were left holding two tiny pieces.

They stared at each other for a shocked moment, then started laughing all over again.

"What am I missing?"

Reggie's smooth voice interrupted their laughter. He stood in the doorway, dressed casually in jeans and an open sports shirt and carrying a thin box. His perfect white teeth flashed as he took in the messy kitchen.

"I'm cooking," Heather explained, going toward him to give him a kiss.

"We had a few . . . experiments," Jake put in.

Reggie set down the box and glanced at the amoeba pizza. "I can see that."

He opened the box and displayed a perfect pizza with artfully arranged vegetables spiraling around the edge. "I stopped at the Tuscan Oven and Mario made this especially for us. All we have to do is pop it into the oven."

"Oh," Heather said in a small voice.

Reggie slipped his arms around her. "You're so cute to try and cook for me, sugar." He kissed the tip of her nose. "But that's why there are chefs."

With a quick motion, he swept Heather and Jake's attempts at pizza off the counter and dumped them into the garbage. He popped the gourmet pizza into the already warm oven and set the timer.

"I'd better get going," Jake said, starting for the door.

"Stay and have pizza with us, Jake," Heather urged. "You deserve a reward for being my assistant."

"There's plenty of pizza," Reggie offered.

"Thanks anyway. I have a patient to check on. Have fun." Jake ducked out the door. A moment later, they heard the front door slam.

Reggie took her in his arms. "I thought he'd never leave," he teased, nuzzling her neck. "I like your roommates, Heather, but do they have to live here?"

Heather smiled. But she hoped that Jake hadn't felt uncomfortable. As much as she liked being alone with her boyfriend, she wished that Jake still socialized with them. Soon after she and Reggie had started dating, Jake's friendship with Reggie had cooled.

Maybe it was because Reggie was now working for his parents' company. He was a marketing genius, according to his mother. Jake's world was completely different—the world of an overburdened, understaffed public hospital. Of course, that was Heather's world, too. Still, she wished that Jake's schedule would allow him to let people into his life instead of shutting them out.

But then Reggie slowly trailed his lips from her earlobe to the back of her neck, and she forgot about Jake. She let out a small sound of pleasure and nestled closer to Reggie.

"Wouldn't it be nice," he murmured in the silky way that turned her bones to water, "if it could be like this all the time?"

Heather nodded dreamily against his chest.

"It can be," he said, stroking her. "It's all up to you, sweetheart."

Heather knew what Reggie was driving at. He'd hinted at their getting married before.

But she wasn't sure if he was one hundred percent serious, number one. Reggie used to be a dating machine at Moorhouse College. Could he really settle for just one girl?

Not to mention that as crazy as she was about the guy, she didn't know if she was ready to get married. She was graduating next week, and she was looking forward to working without the pressure of classes on top of it. Marriage felt like just another pressure right now. She needed time.

Heather frowned. For months now, she'd been telling Reggie that she couldn't even think about marriage until graduation. At the time, it had seemed like a safe thing to say, with the end of her studies looming as a distant, golden, untouchable goal.

But the days and weeks and exams and papers had passed. And suddenly, graduation was only a few days away.

Two

 On graduation day, Heather woke early and turned to gaze out the window at a clear blue sky. She stretched, smiling. She knew it could be her last moment to reflect before the festivities began.

It was hard to believe that the day was finally here. She'd worked hard, concentrating so much on papers and work that she hadn't had a chance to lift her head and look around at her life in a while.

Heather stretched again, yawning luxuriously. What was there to worry about? She had a wonderful boyfriend, a great family, and a fascinating career ahead of her. Life was good.

"All I need is my morning caffeine and it will be perfect," she murmured out loud.

Just then, her nostrils flared as she picked up the scent of rich coffee. Heather grinned. Sherri had flown in late last night from New York City for her graduation. She must have started the coffee.

A knock came at her door and a moment later Sherri's lively face poked around it. "You awake?"

Heather nodded. "Almost."

"Good." Sherri pushed open the door with her hip. "Because I have some serious breakfast here."

Heather rose on her pillows with a cry of pleasure. Sherri was carrying a loaded tray with two cups of steaming coffee and two plates piled with fluffy scrambled eggs, crisp bacon, and toasted bagels.

"I brought the bagels from New York," Sherri said, plunking down the tray. "I thought you deserved breakfast in bed, Miss Master of Social Work."

"This is great," Heather said. She grinned at Sherri as she picked up her fork. "Where's yours?"

Sherri whipped a fork out of the pocket of her robe. "If you think you're eating all this by yourself, you've got another think coming, Johnson."

She waggled onto the bed next to Heather. For a minute, the only sounds were the sipping of coffee and the crunching of bacon.

"So, let's review the day," Sherri said. "Your parents arrive at 9:30, right?"

Heather nodded as she took a bite of scrambled eggs. "They're taking a cab from the airport with Talia. Her flight's scheduled to arrive a half hour earlier."

"And what about that hunky roommate of yours? Is he coming to the ceremony?"

Heather gulped down her coffee in surprise. "You think Jake is a hunk?"

Sherri's eyes widened. "Are you blind?" she asked, around a mouthful of eggs.

"Wait until you see Reggie," Heather said. "He'll be at the ceremony, too. Can you make it to lunch with all of us afterward?"

Sherri shook her head. "I wish I could. But my interview is at two."

Sherri now had her degree in industrial design. She had a position with a firm in New York City, but she was being courted by a prestigious firm for a job right here in Atlanta.

Heather frowned. "How does Marc feel about moving here if you get the job?"

Sherri ran her finger around her coffee cup. "My understanding husband is all for it. I'm the one with reservations. Even if it's the most terrific opportunity in the world, Marc will have to quit his job. And he loves it. He's really going places at his firm.''

''Sounds like a problem,'' Heather said.

Sherri shook her head. ''Not really. I still have a great job in New York, if I decide to stay. And if it *is* a problem, Marc and I will work it out together, the way we always do. He's the best.''

Heather smiled. ''You guys are so good together. It gives the rest of us poor slobs hope.''

Sherri snatched a piece of bacon from Heather's plate. ''The water's fine,'' she said innocently. ''Thinking about jumping in?''

Heather hesitated. ''I don't know.''

''You said you thought Reggie would pop the question after graduation,'' Sherri pointed out. ''Don't you think you should figure out your answer?''

Heather sighed. She took another sip of coffee. ''Don't you think I should *know* the answer?'' she asked.

Within an hour, Heather's small apartment was filled with laughter and confusion. Her parents arrived, along with her sister Talia, whose merry, infectious laugh was soon ringing through the apartment.

Davis and Callie Johnson had taught two things to their children: excellence and service. They'd been taught to give back to their community and to achieve. But the Johnsons also instilled a love for living in their children. Callie and Davis had always run a fun-loving household, full of music and laughter and joy and conversation.

Jake returned from his shift at the hospital, and the Johnsons swept him into the chaotic second breakfast Sherri was organizing. Luckily, she had brought plenty of bagels.

The doorbell pealed twice with presents for Heather. Her brother Nate, who worked in the mayor's office in New York City, sent a huge bouquet of spring flowers. Her brother Douglass, a college professor in New Jersey, sent a bound edition of the plays of August Wilson.

Heather took a quiet moment to read Douglass's inscription on the flyleaf. He had lifted a quote from Wilson:

All you need in the world is love and laughter. That's all anybody needs. To have love in one hand, and laughter in the other.

Heather hugged the book to her. Her family was eating and laughing in the next room, and now it felt like her tall, teasing brothers were there as well.

If only Reggie was there, too! He was supposed to meet her family this morning, but he'd called to cancel. He had a meeting he couldn't miss, he'd told her. But he would be right there in the first row, watching her get her diploma.

Heather held out her hand for the diploma. It slid into her palm and her fingers curled around it.

Done!

She was beaming as she headed back to her seat. Her mother was crying, as usual. Even her father looked misty-eyed. Jake was applauding, and Sherri and Talia were calling out "Go, girl!"

But where was Reggie?

Anxiously, Heather scanned the seats. There was no sign of him. She sat down again, feeling irritated at Reggie. How could he have missed her big day?

Throughout the rest of the ceremony, Heather couldn't concentrate. She kept twisting and turning to see if she could catch sight of Reggie. Her irritation turned to worry. Reggie *wouldn't* miss her big day. Something must have happened!

Finally, the speeches were over and the ceremony ended. Heather headed toward her friends and family.

Jake was the first to reach her. "Way to go, girl," he said, embracing her in a warm bear hug. "I knew you were destined for great things. As long as we kept you out of the kitchen.''

"Thanks a lot, Dr. D," she said with a laugh. "I'll remember that next time you're begging for a fresh pot of coffee.''

"Hey, Master Heather!" Talia cried, kissing her cheek. "Do we have to kneel before you now?"

She was nudged away by Heather's mother. "We're so proud or you, baby." Her arms closed around Heather in a secure, loving hug.

Heather returned their hugs and kisses, but her mind was screaming.

Where is Reggie?

"Where is that boyfriend of yours?" her father asked her. He didn't look too pleased. Heather saw her mother give him a nudge so that he wouldn't press the point. Jake's face was stormy. Sherri and Talia exchanged concerned glances.

Embarrassment surged through her. Heather decided grimly that if Reggie *hadn't* been in a traffic accident, or if he *wasn't* sitting by the hospital bedside of a really close relative, he was dead meat.

"Gosh, what a gorgeous day," Sherri said brightly. "Atlanta is really growing on me."

"It's a great city," Talia said. "I worked at a station here when I was just starting out."

Talia was a television reporter in Baltimore. Sherri turned to her in an obvious attempt to distract everyone from Heather's worried face. "You have to move pretty often if you choose that career," she said. "Is it hard?"

"Sometimes," Talia said. "But I enjoy challenges. And . . ." She went on, but Heather couldn't focus on the words. How could Reggie let her down on such an important day? In front of her friends and family and God and . . .

Heather was scanning the sea of faces when a familiar swagger caught her eye. Worry and embarrassment changed to relief.

Reggie made his way through the crowd in his usual unhurried, graceful fashion. Heather wished he didn't look so handsome in his beautifully cut gray suit. Relief left in a rush and anger flooded in.

Talia and Sherri let out a low whistle at exactly the same moment.

"That man is *fine*," Talia murmured.

"Wow," Sherri breathed.

Reggie smiled as he moved toward them. "Sorry I'm late," he said, bending over to kiss Heather's cheek. "I had something to take care of. It took longer than I thought."

He turned to Heather's parents. "You must be Heather's folks. I'm so pleased to meet you at last."

Her father gave his hand reluctantly to Reggie, and her mother's smile was strained.

No way was Heather going to let this one pass. She opened her mouth to ask him what could possibly have been so important, but the loud buzzing of a plane distracted her.

Then, Reggie looked up with a broad grin. He wasn't paying attention to her at all!

Heather tilted her head back. A plane was flying directly over them, a banner trailing behind it. She gasped as the words registered:

Heather—Please Marry Me—Reggie

Her gaze whipped back to him. His dark eyes were serious now. Her irritation dropped away along with the crowd around her. There was only Reggie.

He took her hand. "I can't live without you, Heather. I knew it from the beginning—this is real love. This is it. Will you marry me?"

Heather felt dazzled. By the blue sky, the sunlight, the bright red banner. By the sheer exhilaration and drama of the proposal. This man would always dazzle her, always sweep away confusion with his confidence and his smile.

Of *course* she had to marry him!

Heather threw herself in his arms, and he caught her against him, his arms strong and capable.

"Yes," she told him, laughing and crying at once. "Yes, yes, yes!"

Then Reggie laughed, too, and Sherri let out a whoop of joy. *With love in one hand and laughter in the other,* Heather thought. Her older brother was right, as usual. Not to mention prophetic!

Three

Later that day, Heather walked Sherri
to the curb to wait for her taxi to the
airport.

"What a day," Sherri said with a sigh. "I get offered
a job that will completely uproot my life, and you get
engaged. Major life changes, girlfriend."

"But good ones," Heather pointed out, smiling.
"What did Marc say about the job?"

"He said he knew I'd get it, and he's ready to move
if I want it," Sherri said. A twinkle lit her eyes. "That
rat."

"So you have a big decision," Heather said. "Of
course I want you to take it, for selfish reasons."

"I know," Sherri said. "It would be great to live in
the same city again. But there's Marc to consider, too. I
know I'd be tearing him away from a job he loves. Not
to mention the fact that both of our families are in New
York. I just don't know, Heather." Sherri hit her own
forehead comically. "When did life get so *serious?*"

"I wish you could stay longer." Heather sighed.
"Maybe we could figure it out if we talked all night."

"We could try," Sherri said. "But at the risk of making you gag, I really miss Marc."

"It's been at least twenty-six hours since you saw him
last," Heather teased.

Sherri laughed. "I know, I know." She hugged

Heather. "Pretty soon, you'll know exactly how I feel."

Heather drew back to look into her friend's face. "Do you really like Reggie?"

Sherri put a finger to her forehead. "Let me think. He's gorgeous, sweet, and smart. He just happens to be fabulously wealthy. And he adores you. There's only one drawback, Heather. I hate to use this horrible word, but . . ."

"What?" Heather prompted nervously.

"He's perfect," Sherri stage-whispered, and they both burst out laughing.

"Not quite," Heather said. "He doesn't cook." Her smile faded, and she sighed. "And my parents aren't thrilled."

"I noticed," Sherri said. "What happened while I was at my interview?"

"They said they liked him very much," Heather told her. "My dad was impressed that Reggie asked him for my hand. They went for a long walk together before Reggie went back to the office. But—"

"—they think you're too young," Sherri supplied.

"Bingo," Heather said. "And I can't argue the point, really. But Reggie is really anxious to be settled. I think it has to do with his brother Geoffrey. He's only a year older than Reggie, and they've always had this competitive thing. Geoffrey has this perfect wife, and this great house, *and* he's a vice president of the company. I think Reggie is tired of feeling like a little brother. He thinks this will get his life going."

Sherri frowned. "Doesn't sound like a good reason to get married to me."

"Oh, I didn't mean it to sound that way," Heather rushed to assure her. "Of course it's not a reason to get married. But it *is* a reason not to wait, if he's sure he's met the right girl."

"And you've met the right guy?"

"Absolutely," Heather said.

"Glad to hear it," Sherri said as the cab pulled up

with a short honk. She shouldered her overnight bag. "Because you're going to have to hold on to that. Marriage is an adventure—the wildest ride of all. Mark my words, you're in for a bumpy road." Her eyes danced. "At least your fiancé has a great car!"

That evening, Heather pressed against the door of Reggie's BMW. She eyed the lovely spring evening nervously. If only she could be out there enjoying it!

Because she wanted to be doing anything but this. Anything but introducing her family to her new in-laws.

When Reggie had called to ask the Johnsons over for dinner at his parents' house, she couldn't think of a reason to refuse. After all, they'd all soon be family. But her parents and the Tylers were so different. They couldn't possibly get along.

What made matters worse was that she sensed Reggie was edgy, too. His nerves were affecting all of them. He kept glancing at his watch, and he'd herded them out of Heather's apartment without letting them finish their iced teas.

"Sorry to rush you folks," he said with a hurried, charming smile, "but my mother insists on punctuality for dinner."

When Heather asked how his parents had reacted to the news, Reggie only said "they're cool." Hardly a rave. Heather began to wonder how welcome she would be in the Tyler home.

And when Heather had greeted Reggie at the door in her flowered print dress with the full skirt, he'd frowned and told her he'd hoped she'd choose her navy linen, since it was dressier. When she'd offered to change, he'd said that they didn't have time.

And if he wasn't driving so fast right now, she'd jump right out the door! She'd run all the way back to her apartment, get into her oldest, coziest jammies, and microwave some popcorn. She and Jake would turn on an old movie . . .

For the last few blocks, the houses had been growing grander and grander. Now, Reggie turned into a long, curving driveway. A huge brick mansion appeared through the trees.

"Whoa," Talia murmured.

Reggie pulled his BMW up behind a Mercedes coupe and a red Miata. "Looks like everybody's here," he said.

Heather swallowed. "Good," she croaked.

Reggie led the way. He gave a short ring, then opened the heavy front door with the intricate brass knocker. He ushered them down the hallway with the thick Oriental runner setting off polished wood floors. Crystal glittered behind a heavy oak breakfront. Reggie swung open the double doors to the living room.

Across an expanse of polished floor and more Oriental rugs, Ruby and Andrew Tyler sat on a brocade couch. Hung over their heads was what Heather thought was a real Picasso. Reggie's younger sister Adrienne lounged in an armchair. His brother Geoffrey and his wife Brianna sat on a smaller matching couch.

Heather saw their gazes sweep over her sister and her parents. She felt her face flush. Talia was dressed in a becoming apricot silk dress, but her parents hadn't brought dressy clothes. She could see Ruby Tyler's eyes narrow as she took in Callie Johnson's schoolteacher attire—a print skirt and a matching red linen blazer.

Heather's chin lifted. She wasn't about to apologize for her parents. Not even to her future mother-in-law.

Reggie hurried forward and made the introductions. Adrienne offered Heather languid congratulations. Geoffrey shook everyone's hand, and Brianna bubbled to Heather how exciting it was. Reggie's father gave her a hug. And Ruby Tyler didn't say anything.

Oh, she said "pleased to meet you and "so glad you could come" to the Johnsons. She even kissed Heather on the cheek with stone-cold lips. But it was perfectly clear to Heather that she wasn't pleased at the news of the engagement. The Johnsons had been in the room for barely five minutes, and they'd failed to pass inspection.

A maid passed around hors d'oeuvres while they all struggled to make stilted conversation. It was agonizing to Heather. Even Talia, a newswoman used to talking to anyone about anything, seemed frozen. And they hadn't even reached the dinner table yet!

"When are you two thinking of tying the knot?" Heather's father asked in one of the many long pauses.

Reggie took Heather's hand. "As soon as possible. This summer for sure."

"Impossible," Ruby said with a chilly laugh. "You can't pull together a wedding in that amount of time."

"Depends on the wedding, I think," Heather's mom said mildly.

"Not a *Tyler* wedding," Ruby declared. "Why, the best caterers are booked at least six months in advance."

"It took a year to plan our wedding," Geoffrey said. "If you want the best, it takes time. Of course, you could always go down to city hall."

Reggie scowled at his brother. "We don't have to do that. We can figure something out."

Ruby Tyler didn't bother to reply. She turned to Heather's father. "Tell me, Mr. Johnson. Are you from California originally?"

"Please, call me Davis," Heather's father answered amiably. "Actually, I grew up in Baltimore, and I still have family there. I've traced our branch of the Johnsons back to before the Civil War. We were slaves in South Carolina. I'm the first member of my family to graduate from college."

"I see," Ruby said. "And you, Mrs. Johnson?"

"Callie," Heather's mom said in her friendly way. But Heather could tell that her mother was barely holding on to her politeness.

Hold on, Mom, Heather pleaded silently. *Please don't lose it with Ruby Tyler.*

"I'm a native Californian," Callie Johnson answered

in a pleasant tone. "But my family is from Massachusetts. Boston, mostly. One of my ancestors fought in the Revolutionary War."

Ruby sat up a little straighter. "Oh?"

"And one fought in the Civil War," Callie continued. "Won the Medal of Honor. My great great great—or is it great great?—grandfather was among the first black men to graduate from Harvard."

Heather let out a slow, relieved breath. What her mother said was all true. And it had impressed Ruby Tyler.

"What about your family, Ruby?" Callie asked.

"We hail from Georgia and Mississippi," Ruby said quickly. "But my, what a distinguished heritage." She beamed an approval at Reggie. "Beauty, brains, and breeding, Reginald. Well done."

Heather should have been happy. But she was tempted to ask her future mother-in-law if Reggie was getting a fiancée—or a horse.

"Maybe it *can* be done this summer," Ruby said later, as they exited the dining room and headed to the living room for coffee and dessert.

"I heard that Cole Bodine broke his engagement," Adrienne piped up. Her brown eyes gleamed in her thin, pretty face. "Serves that snotty Jessica Walker right. They had booked the church and the caterers and everything."

"That means there might be a slot opening up," Ruby mused. "When were they getting married?"

Adrienne shrugged as she plucked the petal off a flower. "Sometime in July."

"It doesn't give us much time," Ruby said. "But still, it's before everyone leaves for August. Now, let me think."

"Mother, this is ridiculous," Geoffrey said. "What about flowers, and the band—"

"And the honeymoon," Reggie said in an undertone to Heather. She hid her smile.

Ruby waved her hand. "Everything can be accomplished if you spread around enough money, darling. Surely business has taught you that by now."

"It's true," Reggie said. "Even the most impossible deadline can be met if you're focused."

His mother and father both smiled at him, and Reggie glowed.

"Then it's settled," Ruby said. "Tomorrow I'll make some calls and find out where the Bodine-Walker wedding was going to be. I'm sure Gladys Walker booked the crème de la crème for Jessica. If we're lucky, we can just slide into her slot."

Heather met her mother's raised eyebrow. She knew what her parents were thinking. It was their responsibility to pay for the wedding. They couldn't afford what Ruby was planning.

Reggie tugged on her hand as they moved toward the living room. While the rest filed in, he steered her out to the terrace.

He took her in his arms. "I just had to be alone with you. It's almost over, sugar. You did great. I'm so proud of you. You're so beautiful and smart and perfect—"

He leaned over and kissed her. Heather felt herself giving in to the tug of Reggie's slow magic, but she resisted.

She pulled away. "Reggie, your mother is making all these plans for the wedding. She didn't once ask what *we* wanted."

"Don't worry about a thing," Reggie murmured. "Mama loves projects. She's just getting carried away. Putting on a wedding in only two months is the biggest project of all. I'll talk to her. Now come here."

Heather found herself melting under the force of Reggie's soft voice and gentle hands. She nestled against him and sighed as his mouth closed over hers. All her worries and frustrations dissolved in the sweet honey of his kiss.

What was she worrying about? A few wedding compromises? A little family tension? Boil down all the petty problems and there was only one thing that mattered, one thing that would carry them through the rest of their lives . . .

Love.

Four

At the airport a few days later, Heather waited with her parents for their flight to be called. Talia had left the day after graduation, since she had to get back to work.

Her father kept jumping up for magazines and drinks of water and to check on the flight information board. Heather and her mother exchanged sympathetic smiles. Davis Johnson was afraid to fly, but he didn't let that stop him from getting on a plane.

"He'll be okay after takeoff," Heather's mother mused. "And I know he's looking forward to getting to Baltimore."

Davis Johnson was taking early retirement from his teaching position next month. He had saved enough money to start on his lifelong dream: a book about the lives of free blacks in the South before the Civil War. Davis and Callie were traveling to Baltimore not only to visit their second daughter, but for Davis to investigate the research possibilities there.

The flight was called, and Callie looked around anxiously for Davis. "Wouldn't you know it," she said. "He's disappeared."

"You still have time, Mom," Heather reassured her.

"And this will give us a chance to say goodbye," her mother said. "I know I'll be seeing you again inside of two months for the wedding. But . . ."

Her mother's eyes filled with tears, and Heather felt her own grow moist. "I know."

Her mother enveloped her in a fierce hug. "I'm so proud of my daughter."

Tears ran down Heather's face as her mother rocked her. A feeling of homesickness swept over her. She'd made a home here in Atlanta. But she missed this feeling.

Her mother drew away so that she could look into Heather's face. Her dark eyes were intent on hers. "Tell me one thing, child. You always knew what you wanted. I'll only ask this one time, so you be honest now. Are you sure?"

Mom didn't have to say any more than that. Heather saw all the uncertainty in her face. She knew what her mother was really asking.

Can you live that kind of life? Can you stand to have dinner with those Tylers every Friday night? Can you handle that Ruby in your face as your mother-in-law?

But what could Heather say? "I love him, Mom," she said helplessly.

Callie reached out and touched her cheek. "Then that's all that matters, baby."

Later that morning, Heather hurried down the halls of the hospital. She had a million things to take care of, and a long list of patients to see. Her day would be crammed with crises and problems and frustrations.

She loved every minute of it.

Heather's position as a patient advocate at the city hospital was a new one. It had been started on an experimental basis, and the hospital and the city were currently trying to come up with a way to finance her position full time. Heather felt confident that it would happen. Her supervisors at both Social Services and the hospital had practically given her a green light.

Health care for indigents as well as normal patients had become more confusing than ever. It was Heather's job to help a confused and sometimes frightened patient cope with the maze of city regulations and social services. This could include anything from filling out insurance forms, to arranging for post-operative in-home care, to making sure the patient talked to the dietician about meal preferences.

Heather loved working within the health care system. She felt as though she was giving back part of her heart and mind to society. The hospital had its share of frustrations. Everyone was overworked. But every day Heather saw courage and hope. And she had doctors like Jake Deveraux to work with, where she got to see dedication up close.

It had only been in the last six months that Heather and Jake had patients in common. One of them was now Heather's secret favorite. Algernon Stokes was a bright, funny five-year-old who had been diagnosed with leukemia.

Heather spotted Jake up ahead, scribbling on a chart as he walked. He was always doing two things at once—except when he was with a patient. Then his entire attention was focused on the problem at hand.

Heather hurried to catch up with him. "Dr. Deveraux!"

He turned. Jake rarely smiled when he was at work, so she wasn't hurt when he responded with a harried frown. "Heather. How's it going?"

"I wanted to discuss the Stokes case with you."

"Step into my office," he said, gesturing at the staff lounge with a slight grin. "I'll buy you a cup of coffee."

As Jake poured the coffee and added a half-packet of sugar and a drop of milk, just the way Heather liked it, she filled him in on her concerns.

"I can see that Algie's doing well," she told Jake. "My concern is Crystal."

Jake frowned. "His mother?"

"She just got a job at an import-export company," Heather explained. "She's been spending so much time here that she's afraid she'll be fired. She just got the job, Jake. It was a new start for them. You know she's a single parent.''

Jake nodded as he took a sip of coffee. "But Algie's improving," he said.

"That's part of the problem," Heather said. "What I mean is, he's going to need in-home care for a few weeks, right?"

"Maybe not that long," Jake said.

"If Crystal gets fired, she'll lose her insurance," Heather explained. It was a typical, sad case for Heather—struggling families caught in the cracks of the system.

She waited a beat, watching Jake's face. When she first got this job, it amazed her that doctors focused on the patient's disease and didn't know much about the personal situations. Now she knew that doctors were overloaded with cases, and they *had* to focus. Part of her job was getting them to see that occasionally they had to take into account other less tangible factors than diagnosis and treatment.

"I'd hate to see someone like Algie lose private insurance," Jake mused. "He's going to need care for some time. I have the best of hopes, but it could be a long haul."

"What I'm thinking is, if you could keep him here for an extra day or two, I'd have time to arrange home care with Crystal. She thinks she can round up some neighbors to help."

Jake nodded slowly. "I think I can do that. We have some empty beds at the moment."

"Great," Heather said crisply. "Algie's mom is the key to his recovery, you know."

"I thought it was my awesome medical skills," Jake said.

She looked up from her coffee and saw he was teasing. "Let's just say you're a team," she answered, smiling.

They sipped their coffee, enjoying the quiet moment. Heather was dying to ask Jake what he thought about her engagement. He'd left so abruptly after Reggie's dramatic proposal. Since then she'd been busy with her parents, so they hadn't had a chance to talk.

She wanted his blessing. He was one of her best friends. But she didn't want to ask for it! She was almost a little annoyed that she had to prompt him.

"So what do you think of my news?" she finally asked, keeping the exasperation out of her voice. "You haven't said a word."

Jake turned away to pick up his chart. "Congratulations, of course," he said.

He leaned over and gave her a swift kiss on the cheek. For one instant, Heather felt the touch of his lips and remembered what it had felt like to *really* kiss him. Jake had always checked his passion. Still, she had felt it there, behind the few sweet kisses they'd shared.

But Jake pulled away before she could completely register the memory. She returned to reality and the small, cluttered staff lounge with a bump.

Jake studied his chart for a moment. "So how does Reggie feel about your staying on at the hospital?"

Surprised, Heather put down her coffee cup. "What do you mean? He thinks it's great."

Jake gave a reluctant shrug. "I'm probably off base. I always thought Reggie was the old-fashioned type. He used to say he wanted a real wife. All that social stuff—entertaining, country clubs. . . . His kind of life demands it."

Heather laughed. "Wake up, Jake. It's the nineties. Reggie knows how important my career is to me."

Jake's beeper went off. "Gotta motor," he said. But he hesitated. "Heather, I'm sorry I mentioned it. I'm sure you're right. Catch you later, okay? Keep me updated on the Stokes problem."

Heather nodded, and Jake hurried off in his long-legged stride. She picked up her coffee again and sipped it.

Jake was wrong, of course. Maybe Reggie had made some sort of offhand comment once that Jake had misinterpreted. She knew her career was important to him.

But Jake's words sent a chill through her. She knew how much Reggie admired his mother. And Brianna didn't work. Did Reggie want a wife just like his mother and sister-in-law? A wife who would create a beautiful home and attend the right clubs?

Heather drained her coffee. She knew that Jake was wrong, and she was right. But maybe it was time she asked Reggie a few pointed questions about how he viewed their future.

Five

Heather was hoping for some quiet time with Reggie that evening, but he'd already made special plans. A new restaurant had opened in Atlanta, an old-fashioned supper club with dancing, and they were meeting Reggie's friends there.

Heather didn't know Reggie's crowd very well. They were part of the young African-American elite of Atlanta. They'd grown up together and had gone to the same parties and charity functions all their lives. They were a fun-loving crowd, always ready to try a new restaurant or go dancing, and she was looking forward to getting to know them. If only she felt that she had something in common with them.

The restaurant was decorated in white shimmering fabrics, even on the walls. Tiny candles in blue glass holders flickered on the tables. Reggie's crowd had commandeered a large table at the rear. Reggie's best friend Paul Charvet stood and waved them over.

As they approached, Heather saw that Reggie's sister Adrienne was among the group. She had saved two seats for Heather and Reggie. Next to Adrienne was a pretty, slender girl Heather had never seen before.

"Reggie, you remember my friend Yolanda, don't you?" Adrienne said, leaning over to talk to him. "She moved up North when I was in high school."

"Sure I do," Reggie said. "Skinny little thing with matchstick legs and braces on her teeth?"

The petite girl giggled, and Adrienne poked Reggie. "This is her, big mouth. She's here for the summer, staying with her aunt and uncle. She's a junior at Connecticut College."

Reggie gave a long, slow look at Yolanda. Heather remembered that look. She'd gotten it the first night she'd met Reggie, when he'd come to the apartment to pick up Jake for a basketball game.

"No way, sister. This isn't Yolanda. This is some stranger pulling a con on you," Reggie said.

Adrienne played impatiently with her silverware. "Reggie, I'm telling you—"

"This woman is way too fine to be that scragglehaired stick," Reggie went on. He teasingly peered under the table. "And those aren't matchstick legs, no way."

Yolanda giggled again. The sound was beginning to grate on Heather's nerves. She wasn't bothered—too much—that Reggie was flattering a friend of his baby sister. But did Yolanda have to keep giggling that way?

Reggie looked around. "I think I'd better call the maitre d'. He should throw this woman out, because it sure isn't Yolanda."

"Reggie, stop it," Adrienne said delightedly. Yolanda seemed incapable of stringing words together in a sentence. She didn't have to. She had a luscious, pampered prettiness that Heather knew was just Reggie's type. She ducked her head, her hair swinging. To Heather's satisfaction, she saw that Yolanda's ears were rather large for her small head. At least the girl had a flaw.

Reggie's friend Paul leaned across the table. "Hey, Reg. What's all this I hear about a house for you?"

Startled, Heather wrenched her attention from Yolanda to look at Reggie.

Reggie's grin was broad. "Thanks, bro. You just blew my surprise."

Paul's fiancée Suzanne swatted him. "Big mouth."

Heather plastered a smile on her face. "What house, Reggie?"

"It's Mama," Reggie told her. "She decided my condo was too small." He turned to the rest of the table. "Ruby found out that big white house on Glen Trace was coming up for sale—the Baldwins are getting divorced. She went right up to Mrs. Baldwin and made her an offer. 'You kids have to start out right,' " Reggie finished, mimicking his mother affectionately.

"The Baldwin house?" Suzanne breathed. "Lucky you, Heather. It has one of those gorgeous black-bottomed pools. And what, five bedrooms?"

Heather spoke in an undertone to Reggie. "We can't afford something like that."

"Don't worry, sugar. I worked it out with Mom. They're putting up the down payment. All we have to do is come up with the mortgage payment, and that will be less than our combined rents." He patted her arm. "I've got it all figured out."

"But what about insurance and upkeep?" Heather asked. She knew she was asking the wrong question. What she really wanted to ask was *what about what I want?*

Adrienne clapped her hands. "That's fabulous! It's only a few blocks from our house."

"And it has those gorgeous white columns," Suzanne said.

"I can use the pool!" Adrienne cried.

"You already have a pool," Reggie pointed out.

"I know, but the Baldwins' is so much nicer," Adrienne said. "Besides, I can wear my string bikini and Mama won't be around to scold me."

Al, one of Reggie's friends from Moorhouse, winked. "In that case, brother, we'll be partying at your house. You won't get lonely."

Adrienne shot a flirtatious glance at Al, and Yolanda giggled again.

Paul smiled at Heather. "Hurricane Ruby strikes again. Now you don't have to worry about a thing."

Everyone looked at her as though she had it made. But Heather just felt strange, as if she was being handed a life she didn't choose.

When the band started to play, the table cleared as everyone got up to dance. Rising, Reggie took her hand, but she resisted his tug.

"Can we just talk for a minute?" Heather asked.

"If it's about the house, don't worry," Reggie said. "Of course I told Mama that you had to see it first."

"It's not the house," Heather said, waving her hand. "I mean, we can talk about that later. I have a question I want to ask you."

Reggie smiled. "I'm all yours."

"Reggie, how do you feel about my job?" she blurted. "I mean, do you mind that I'm going to keep working after we're married?"

Reggie laughed. "What a silly question. Do you think I'm some sort of caveman?"

Heather smiled, relieved. "I just had to be sure."

"What you do is part of you, Heather," Reggie said, squeezing her hand. "I love you and I love how dedicated you are. I'm proud of you, baby."

"Oh, Reggie," she said, leaning against him. "It's just that your world is so different than mine."

"My world *is* your world," Reggie corrected gently. "And your world is mine. That's what marriage is all about."

"Speaking of my world, I had an awful day," Heather said, taking a sip of her soda.

"Poor baby. Tell me about it," Reggie urged.

"It's this case—this little boy Algie. He has leukemia. Oh, Reggie, it's just so heartbreaking. He's so brave and he's trying so hard. And his mom might lose her job if I don't think of something fast—"

Heather's voice trailed off. Reggie's gaze had drifted

to the dance floor. He wasn't listening to her!

"Hey," she said, poking him. "Am I boring you?"

His gaze snapped back to hers. "I'm sorry, sweetheart. I guess I had a rough day, too. Just hearing about your day made me think about mine. And I was trying to forget about it."

"What happened?" she asked in concern.

"Just business," he said, shrugging. "Geoff pulled off this amazing feat today. He probably expanded our market by a third. Dad just about busted every button on his suit. It's good for us, good for the company, but . . ."

"But you're jealous," Heather said gently.

"I can't help it," Reggie said. "He's always one step ahead of me." His dark eyes suddenly lit with a twinkle. "After all, he's better looking and smarter than I am—"

"He is not," Heather said defensively.

Reggie slipped his arms around her. "But at least he won't have a better-looking wife. You're so beautiful, sweetheart."

Heather shifted uncomfortably. She felt strange when Reggie talked about her that way. Sure, it was nice that he found her attractive, but there was so much more to a person than the way they looked. Besides, she was sick of hearing about his brother. Was Reggie marrying her to compete with Geoff?

He kissed her. "But that's not why I love you. You fill my soul, Heather. You *are* my soul. I didn't know I had one until I met you."

She melted against him. Just when she felt unsure, he always said the perfect thing to reassure her.

"Now let me show you off," he said, pulling her to her feet.

She followed him to the dance floor. He held her close, and their bodies moved together perfectly, the way they had from the very beginning.

It felt so *right*. Heather felt herself relax. She closed her eyes and held Reggie closer.

If I ever wonder if this is right, I just have to think about this moment, she decided.

Because Heather's bumpy road loomed ahead. Tomorrow, she had a date to look at wedding gowns—with Hurricane Ruby, her future mother-in-law.

Six

 *It's really nice of Ruby to offer to do this,* Heather told herself on Saturday morning. *My mom's in California and my sister is in Baltimore. I need another woman's help to pick out a dress. No question.*

"I thought we'd drive by the church, so you can see it," Ruby said, piloting her Mercedes expertly through Atlanta's suburban streets.

"I didn't realize we'd picked a church," Heather said, surprised. "Reggie didn't mention it."

Ruby laughed. "It's not a question of *picking,* dear. Only one church is appropriate for Reggie's wedding."

Reggie's wedding? What am I, invisible?

"I go to a Baptist church near my apartment," Heather said. "It's small and covered with ivy—"

"I'm sure that would have been sweet, Heather," Ruby said, pulling over in front of a soaring glass and stone structure. "Isn't it dramatic? You should see the altar. Acres of Italian marble. Reggie was baptized here. And there are plenty of pews for a large wedding."

"Very dramatic," Heather said politely.

Ruby pulled the Mercedes into traffic again. "Now for the gown."

The Tylers are paying for most of the wedding. And my church probably is too small. Ruby is just being practical. And it was sweet of her to offer to bring me

40

today. I'm sure she has a billion better things to do with her Saturday. She might seem like a tyrant. But Reggie's right—she's really a marshmallow.

Really.

"This will give us a chance to talk about what you want for the wedding," Ruby said. "Thank goodness everything worked out with the caterer and the club. Any ideas on the ceremony?"

You see? She's interested in what I think!

"I was thinking of incorporating some African elements into the ceremony," Heather said eagerly. "Jumping the broom—"

"Broom? In Saint Michael's?"

"And maybe I'd wear a gown with a sash or a stole of *kente* cloth."

Ruby's polished fingernails tapped on the steering wheel. "Whatever for, dear?"

"Because it's part of my heritage," Heather said. "And I'm proud of it. Weddings are about tradition, aren't they?"

"I agree," Ruby said. "And the *Tyler* tradition is rooted in Atlanta. I think all this newfangled emphasis on our African roots is ridiculous. We're *Americans*."

"Well—" Heather started faintly.

"Now," Ruby said firmly, "do you have anything in mind for the food?"

See? She's still interested in what you want, isn't she?

"I was thinking of including some Caribbean dishes," Heather admitted. "First of all, I love spicy food. And part of my mother's family is from the West Indies."

Ruby took a right turn a little too sharply. "How . . . ethnic," she said. "I had salmon and champagne in mind."

"That sounds nice," Heather said politely. "But we could have something like jerk chicken for folks who like spicy food."

"Jerk chicken," Ruby repeated, as though Heather

had just said *fried cockroaches*. "I can't see Monsieur Antoine preparing something called 'jerk chicken,' Heather. Perhaps you should rethink."

Perhaps I should rethink, is right! Perhaps I should rethink taking you on as a mother-in-law! Perhaps ...

Okay. Okay. Relax. Ruby is from a different generation. She just wants the best for her son. And she's a marshmallow, remember? Underneath that steely exterior beats a heart of pure goo. Reggie swears it's true. So it has to be. Right?

"I was thinking of a long train on the gown," Ruby said. "And silk organza. Definitely organza."

Pure goo, Heather. Just hang in there. You'll find it.

"Perfect," Ruby said. "This is the gown. Don't you agree?"

"I'm not sure ...." Heather said. But Ruby had been speaking to the saleswoman.

"Most definitely," she said.

Heather twisted so she could see the back of the gown in the mirror. It *was* beautiful. No question. But it was so ... *grand.*

The off-the-shoulder white satin bodice had seventeen covered buttons marching up the back. The silk organza skirt was a gauzelike confection that was embroidered in flower patterns with small crystals that caught the light. Attached to the waist at the back was a piece of rich satin, the same material as the bodice, that extended behind her in a train.

"I was thinking of something more ... simple," Heather said.

Ruby fussed around the dress, pulling out the train, smoothing a fold. "It's perfect. Honey, let me give you a piece of advice. In that church, you need this gown."

"I liked the last gown," Heather said. It had been a satin column, sleeveless, with a draped neckline. Just her style.

Ruby shook her head. "It doesn't come close to this."

She turned to the chic saleswoman. "Don't you agree?"

"Absolutely," the saleswoman said, nodding so rapidly Heather was afraid her half-eyeglasses would fly off. "This is the most beautiful gown in our shop."

Not to mention the most expensive, Heather thought wryly. But what could she do? Ruby was actually smiling at her in approval. Heather didn't want to disappoint her.

She looked in the mirror again. Ruby was right—it was an awfully big church. Plenty of room for a six-foot train.

But how was she going to afford this? Her mother wanted to pay for her gown. Her parents felt guilty about the Tylers picking up the tab for the wedding, even though they couldn't afford the big society gala that Ruby demanded.

"Now, don't you worry about the price. It's a present from me, dear," Ruby said. "So you'll be absolute perfection for Reggie."

"I can't accept—" Heather began.

"Of course you can." Ruby eyed her critically. "You have such a lovely skin tone, Heather. Now don't forget to pile on the sunscreen, *always.* I never put a toe out of the house without slathering on 30 SPF. I can get you a tube of what I use. You don't want to get any darker."

Heather bit her lip so that she wouldn't snap at Ruby. If there was one thing that infuriated her, it was the idea that a lighter-skinned black woman was more desirable.

"It's a pity that so many social events in Atlanta are outdoors," Ruby went on. "The annual luncheon of the Oleander Club is coming up, for example. You'll be attending—I'm proposing your name. And you *must* join my book group, the Literati. We meet every Thursday afternoon. It's an easy way to keep up with what's happening in the cultural world—not to mention all the society gossip."

Thursday afternoons? Luncheons? Didn't Ruby realize that she worked for a living?

Ruby stepped back to get a long view of the dress. "Now we'll have to pick out a headdress—something with a veil. And shoes. *Peau de soie,* I think. The Italians do such beautiful work. I know just where to go."

"Ruby—"

"And do you know what we'll be doing right after the wedding?"

"Honeymooning?" Heather guessed.

Ruby laughed. "After that. I'm not coming along on your honeymoon, dear. By the way, I suggest Bermuda. But I don't think Reggie would put up with my joining you."

You never know . . .

"No, I mean *decorating.* I'm already making sketches. I'm a frustrated interior decorator, so be prepared. And I know all the best shops here in Atlanta. We'll have some lovely lunches and then go shopping. You'll love it."

Heather opened her mouth, then shut it. First of all, she wanted Ruby to stop telling her what she was going to do! What clubs she was going to join, what functions she had to attend, even what kind of *shoes* she was going to buy!

And second of all, she wanted to tell Ruby that she'd be working. Did Ruby think she could leave a cancer patient hanging in order to attend a meeting of the Ole-ander Club?

But she'd let Reggie handle that one. His mother was a marshmallow, right? And if Ruby didn't like it, Heather would split and toast her over a roaring fire!

Heather's lips curved in a smile. But it faded when she met her image in the mirror.

Who are you kidding, girl? You're standing there in a dress you don't want. In a little over a month, you'll be walking down the aisle of the biggest, ugliest church you've ever seen. Stand up to Hurricane Ruby? She just flattened you—and there's no disaster relief in sight!

Seven

Heather didn't get a chance to speak to Reggie until late Sunday afternoon, when they had a tennis date with Geoffrey and Brianna. As they strolled to the courts, Heather told him about Ruby's expectations.

Reggie grinned. "Do you think we're the modern Stone Age family, Heather? Mama was just talking. Of course she expects you to work."

"Brianna doesn't work," Heather pointed out.

Reggie frowned. "She doesn't have to. Geoff makes more than I do. Which is a situation I'm going to change."

"Reggie, it doesn't matter how much money you make," Heather said. "I'm still going to work. It's just that . . . well, nothing against your parents. But that's not the kind of life I want." She looked at him searchingly. "What about you?"

Reggie stopped and turned to her. "I want *our* life, Heather. I don't want my parents' life. So stop worrying. Okay?"

She smiled. "Okay."

They continued strolling. Reggie swung his tennis racket as he walked. "You know, honey, if my mother invited you to join the Literati, it's a really good sign. It means she's accepted you. You really shouldn't turn down her offer."

"But Reggie, the book club meets in the afternoons," Heather protested.

"You could probably take an afternoon off once a month," he pointed out.

"My job doesn't work that way," Heather said.

"I'm sure something could be worked out," Reggie said, waving his racket. "And the Oleander Club—most black women in Atlanta would kill for an invitation to join. It's a great way to network."

"But I don't know anything about gardening!" Heather protested.

"Think of it as civic improvement, sugar," Reggie said. "It's all about the beautification of Atlanta."

Great, Heather thought. *Now if I don't join the Oleander Club, I'll be a bad citizen.*

"All my friends' wives and girlfriends are in it," Reggie said. "Even Adrienne is a junior member." He squeezed her arm. "You'll have fun. Trust me."

"I trust you, Reggie," Heather said worriedly. "It's just that . . . all that stuff. It's not *me.*"

Ahead of them, Geoffrey raised his racket in a wave. "You ready to go down in flames?"

"Dream on, bro," Reggie answered with a tight smile.

He turned to her again. "Listen to me, sugar," he said in a soft voice. "Family duties are just a tiny part of what our life will be about." He slipped his arms around her. "*This* is what our life will be about."

Heather's head swam as Reggie kissed her softly. His lips felt like silk, and he tasted like ripe berries. When she leaned back, she saw him silhouetted against the blue sky, his burnished, coppery skin glowing against his tennis whites, his legs strong and muscular, his teeth white and even as he smiled at her.

With a man like that in love with her, Heather thought dizzily, *what could possibly go wrong?*

"Whoa. You all better wait for the honeymoon!" Brianna called teasingly.

Reggie laughed and picked up his racket. "As a mat-

46

ter of fact, I *can't* wait," he murmured to Heather with a smile that stopped her heart.

"The *Oleander* Club?" Corinne let out a shriek. "Give me a break!"

Heather giggled. Just hearing Corinne's laugh made her feel better. She snuggled into the couch and pulled the bowl of popcorn closer. "And the Literati," she said. "We meet Thursday afternoons," she repeated in Ruby's upper-crust accent.

"Right before tea, I'm sure," Corinne said in an amused tone.

"Oh, Corinne, what am I going to do?" Heather asked. "I love Reggie, but his mother is *designed* to drive me bats!"

Corinne laughed again. "What can I say? You just have to hang in. I've been there, remember? And I'm still standing. Wedding preparations are a stress test, but it's all worth it. Married life is so great, Heather. I love Jeff more every day."

"That's what Sherri says," Heather said.

"She loves Jeff more every day?"

"Wise guy," Heather said, laughing.

"Remember when I was having all those problems with Jeff?" Corinne said. "Sherri brought me that picture of us on our backpacking trip. She told me to concentrate on that when things got hairy. It helped. So here's my suggestion: the next time his mother drives you crazy, or you think you're going to lose it, have a mental picture of your love. Find a great memory and hang on to it."

"I wish you were here," Heather said, sighing.

"I'll be there before you know it. And Jeff's coming, too. We'll have a blast. I can't wait to meet Mr. Dreamboat. I heard all about how handsome he was from Sherri. Leave it to you to find the perfect man."

There was that word *perfect* again. Heather sighed.

But she wanted what her friends had—marriages that

worked. Commitments that they could depend on. A man she could have fun with, a man she could trust.

Corinne and Sherri had promised that all her doubts and anxieties were normal, and she believed them. "Focus on what's important," they'd both told her. "Be patient."

Great advice. But how do you learn patience when you're a strong-willed control freak?

her

Eight

 A few weeks later, Heather nervously twisted a curl in front of the mirror at the country club. The ladies' room was full of women in bright summer dresses, laughing and chattering. She didn't know any of them, and they were all there for her engagement party.

She twisted to give herself a critical look. At least she felt she was dressed right. Her simple bronze silk sheath brought out the honeyed tones of her skin and the amber flecks in her eyes. She'd slid a gold cuff on one arm and wore the pretty peridot earrings her parents had given her for her graduation. She'd even worn high heels, which she rarely did. She didn't care if her feet hurt like crazy tomorrow. The heels made her legs look slender and longer than ever. Heather smiled, remembering the approving look in Reggie's eyes when she'd opened her door.

Remembering that look was enough to propel her into the swirling party. She could even face Ruby, Heather decided, lifting her chin and scanning the crowd for Reggie.

All of the elite of Atlanta seemed to be there. Reggie had told her that two players from the Atlanta Braves baseball team were there. And Brianna had pointed out a woman from the city council. But everywhere she looked, Heather hardly registered people. What she noticed was designer dresses and suits, expensive jewelry, and stylish haircuts.

"There you are, Heather." Ruby slipped a slender arm through hers. Her large diamond ring flashed as she waved a greeting at a friend across the room. Dressed in a red shantung silk dress, she looked elegant and beautiful. "I want to introduce you to a few people. Where's Reggie?"

"I haven't seen him since we got here," Heather admitted.

Ruby patted her arm. "That's all right, we won't wait for him."

They began to stroll through the crowd, but suddenly, Ruby leaned forward and squinted at a table in the far corner. "Who are those people? I don't know those people."

Following her gaze, Heather saw that it was a table full of her friends from school and the hospital. She'd even invited some former clients that she'd helped when she'd volunteered at Social Services during her first year at school.

They were all good friends whom Heather felt comfortable with. But most of them looked out of place at this gathering. They'd worn their best clothes, and she was touched by the effort. And she was happy to see that they weren't allowing the opulent country club to dampen their spirits. They all looked as though they were having a wonderful time.

"They're my friends, Ruby," Heather told her.

"I see." Ruby's gaze flicked over them. "Are they *all* invited to the wedding, dear?"

Heather's temper flared, but she tamped it down. "Yes," she said quietly. "And they've all accepted."

"I see," Ruby said again.

The words settled like a stone in Heather's chest. The feeling was starting to be familiar. She'd once again failed her mother-in-law. Her friends weren't grand enough. Heather imagined that tone repeated, over and over, through the years of her marriage. A cold hand seemed to grasp her heart, and she shivered.

"Oh, there's Estella Wentworth," Ruby said. "You *must* meet her. She's one of my oldest and dearest friends."

Heather allowed herself to be pulled along. Everyone welcomed her as if she was already part of the family. She warmed under their interest, and was tickled by the fuss they made over her. *Maybe it wouldn't be so hard to become part of this life after all,* Heather thought.

But while she met people and smiled and made small talk, Heather sneaked looks over the crowd for Reggie. Weren't they supposed to be doing this together? Ruby didn't seem to mind. She just kept saying what a "great mingler" her son was.

But soon even Ruby grew impatient. It didn't help Heather's mood that for the past half hour, every time she spotted Reggie he seemed to be either talking or dancing with Yolanda.

Finally, Ruby led Heather determinedly through the crowd to ambush Reggie.

"Heather! There you are, honey." Reggie slid an arm around her waist. "I missed you," he murmured.

Heather allowed herself to be pulled against him. She didn't like the way Yolanda's big brown eyes shone, and she *especially* didn't care for how pretty the girl looked that evening. She looked slender as a reed in a yellow slip dress that was way too bare, in Heather's opinion. Especially when the girl had her big eyes plastered on Heather's man. At least she'd worn her hair back in a French twist tonight, so her big ears were visible. She probably couldn't resist showing off her dangling earrings in heavy gold.

Heather told herself to stop being jealous. She consoled herself with the happy thought that Yolanda was just a spacy young thing who didn't have enough brains or nerve to string two sentences together.

Yolanda slid her shining gaze from Reggie to his

mother. "Oh, Mrs. Tyler," she purred, "your son has been telling me all about his new house. He says that you're the one who found it. I know the place well. I so admire the classic proportions. It's an elegant marriage of the Italianate style and the Southern vernacular."

Say what?

Ruby looked pleased. "My, Yolanda, you seem to know quite a bit about architecture."

Yolanda cast her eyes down modestly. "I'm an art history major with a concentration in decorative arts," she said. "Last summer I interned at Sotheby's."

"Ah," Ruby said, impressed. "It's so nice to find a young person who cares about such things."

"I care *passionately*," Yolanda said, her dangling earrings vibrating as she shook her head at Ruby. "I just despise the current fashion for old farm furniture. They call an old rickety table with the paint rubbed away 'distressed.' It makes *me* distressed to see it. Give me a good English or French antique—or at *least* a decent reproduction."

"I couldn't agree more!" Ruby cried, pleased.

Heather thought of the old country armoire with the whitewashed paint in her bedroom and winced inwardly. For vases, she collected old pharmaceutical glass bottles in sun-washed colors, or interesting pottery from art fairs. She and Ruby had totally different styles. Decorating the house would be a nightmare of clashing tastes.

As if Ruby had read her mind, she turned to Heather. "I have a fabulous idea. Yolanda, why don't you help Heather out this summer? There's so much to be done with the house."

"I'd be happy to," Yolanda said, blinking sincerely at Heather. "Anytime."

"Don't worry, we'll be calling on you," Reggie said jovially.

Over my dead body, Heather thought.

"Will you excuse me?" she said politely. "I need to say hello to some of my work friends."

"Of course," Yolanda said.

"Don't be long," Reggie said, squeezing her waist. Ruby just waved a manicured hand and turned her attention back to Yolanda.

But instead of heading for her friends, Heather headed for the food. Maybe she was feeling so lost and empty because she *was* empty. Ruby hadn't given her a chance to taste a morsel of food.

Heather stood in front of the buffet table. There were at least six kinds of salads, some sort of poached fish, and shrimp. Thinly sliced beef tenderloin was nestled next to baby vegetables. The delicate food looked gorgeous.

There was only one problem: what she needed was a big, fat enchilada.

A low, amused voice came from directly behind her. "Longing for José's Joint?"

"Jake." Heather turned and smiled at him. "How did you guess? I'd kill for a burrito."

"I'd take you away from all this, but I think your future mother-in-law would kill me," Jake said with a grin.

Heather sighed. "I'm afraid I'm not doing well in that department tonight, anyway," she admitted.

Jake scowled. "From where I sit, they're lucky to get you."

Heather smiled wryly. "Thanks." She eyed his smooth, dark suit. She was so accustomed to seeing him in jeans or sweats or medical whites. Then again, it wasn't every day that Jake saw her in a bronze silk gown. "You clean up nice," she teased.

"Think so?" He touched the knot of his silk necktie. "Personally, I think suits are for stiffs. That's why I went into medicine. Nothing like a baggy old lab coat."

"Eight years of study just for the wardrobe?" she laughed. "Don't let your patients find out." Standing next to him, she noticed that she was eye-to-eye with Jake. Tonight, her high heels made her just as tall as he was. Her grin tilted into mischief. "You can't call me Peanut tonight."

Jake's eyes skimmed her appearance. They warmed with approval and pleasure. "But I can call you beautiful," he said softly.

Embarrassed, Heather dropped her gaze. Jake never gave her compliments. It wasn't that she didn't *like* it. It just made her feel so . . . strange.

"Will you dance with me?" Jake asked, touching her arm.

She raised her eyes again. "Of course."

The band had just struck up a slow, dreamy ballad. Jake led her to the dance floor and she stepped into his arms.

He held her loosely, easily. Heather relaxed for the first time that evening. Their steps moved so smoothly that it felt as if they'd danced together a hundred times before. She knew what he would do before he did it, just from the slight pressure on the small of her back.

Slow and easy, they circled the floor. The music lulled Heather, and she relaxed even more. Jake pulled her the slightest bit closer. Her cheek brushed his shoulder, and she rested it there.

I feel so safe, Heather thought, her eyes half-closed. The room blurred behind her eyelashes. Jake's heartbeat beat against hers. *I wish the music would never end . . .*

"May I cut in?"

Reggie's words were brusque. Jake's arms stiffened, but he didn't let go. He looked into her eyes. "Heather?"

Reggie's spoke through his teeth. "Let her go," he said, forcing out each word like a small, hard pebble.

"Reggie!" Heather spoke softly as she stepped out of Jake's arms. She didn't want to attract attention. She smiled at Jake. "Thank you for the dance."

He nodded curtly. Without even glancing at Reggie, he walked away.

Heather stepped stiffly into Reggie's arms. "What's

the matter with you?'' she said in a low, furious tone. ''Why were you so rude to Jake?''

''He was holding you too close,'' Reggie said, spinning her around.

''First of all,'' Heather said through her teeth, ''he wasn't. And second of all, I'm surprised you could unglue yourself from Yolanda long enough to be able to tell!''

''I'm just trying to make her feel comfortable,'' Reggie protested. ''She's a little shy, and she doesn't know many people here. This is the first summer she's been back since high school.''

''She's about as shy as a barracuda,'' Heather muttered.

''You're jealous,'' Reggie said, smiling. ''That's a good sign, you know.''

''Guess again,'' Heather said.

''Besides,'' Reggie said, spinning her past the band, ''it's different with Jake. You *live* with him. People keep asking me who the handsome, tall guy in the glasses is, and I have to tell them that he's my fiancée's *roommate*. It doesn't sound good, Heather.''

Heather lifted her shoulders in a shrug. ''So don't tell them. Just say he's my friend. *Our* friend.''

The music stopped, and they applauded politely. Reggie drew her away to stand by a pillar, away from the crowd. His expression was grim as he looked at her.

''That's not good enough,'' he said. ''Now that Debbie's moved out, it's not right, you living alone with Jake.''

Heather gazed at him, angry and puzzled. ''What are you talking about, Reggie?''

Reggie's full lips pressed into a thin line. ''He has to move out, Heather. And if you don't ask him, I will!''

55

$\mathcal{N}ine$

 Heather didn't get a chance to argue with Reggie. Every time they had a minute alone, a well-wisher would interrupt them. And Geoff and Brianna drove her home, since it was on their way and Reggie had to get up early for work in the morning.

Heather arrived at the apartment feeling upset and disoriented. She needed to discuss the situation with someone who made sense, someone who knew Reggie.

Jake.

Heather stood in the hall, hesitating. Jake's bedroom door was already closed, and one of the house rules was that if someone's door was closed, it meant they didn't want to be bothered, even for a phone call. They were either deep in concentration over their studies, or asleep. They shouldn't be disturbed unless the house was burning down or the hospital called.

It wasn't even eleven o'clock yet. He *couldn't* be asleep. But Heather sighed and turned away. She'd talk to him tomorrow.

The next day, she rose early and pulled on her running clothes. A good, hard run always restored her perspective. As she ran through the sun-dappled streets, Heather resolved what she would say to Reggie. She'd be logical and firm. And Reggie would relent on this ridiculous request.

Not request. Order, Heather thought, speeding up her pace.

It wasn't like Reggie. But he'd been jealous. Maybe she shouldn't have danced so close to Jake. Heather forced herself to be honest. She would have been jealous, too, if Yolanda had danced so close to Reggie. Even though she felt nothing but friendship for Jake, other people might misinterpret things. Especially in a setting like their engagement party when all eyes were on the bride-to-be, a relative stranger to a very exclusive circle of friends.

Heather jogged up the stairs to her apartment. Jake's door was still closed, so she crept quietly into the kitchen for water. While she swigged a long, cooling swallow from the plastic bottle, she dialed Reggie's number.

Reggie had such a sweet, forgiving heart. He was so kind and giving. Today she'd find out that he'd reconsidered.

But he hadn't.

"Absolutely not," Reggie said smoothly. "Why should I? I'm right about this, Heather. I was hoping you'd see it my way by this morning."

"Reggie, listen to me." Heather took another sip of water from the bottle. "Jake has no money to speak of. I can't ask him to move out, just like that! Look, our wedding is in less than a month. Can't you be patient?"

"I've *been* patient," Reggie said doggedly. "Why can't you understand that I don't want you living with another man?"

"I'm not *living* with him," Heather said. "I'm his roommate. There's a difference. You didn't mind when we were dating!"

"That was different," Reggie returned. "Look, if it's the money, I'll pay Jake's share."

"It's not the money!" Heather snapped. "Haven't you been *listening* to me!"

Reggie's voice shifted into his soothing rumble.

"Look, baby, I'm not trying to be unreasonable. I'm just concerned about what people think."

Heather slammed down the water bottle. "Who cares what people think! I certainly don't. And I'm not asking Jake to move out!"

Just then, Jake appeared in the doorway dressed in an faded black T-shirt and jeans. He rubbed a hand tiredly through his short hair.

"It's okay, Heather," he said quietly. "Reggie is right. I should go."

By that evening, Jake was packed and ready to head out. He had arranged to move in with another intern at the hospital. Derek was glad to exchange his foldout couch for a little extra cash.

Heather helped Jake load the last of his things into Derek's car. While Derek waited behind the wheel, she and Jake said goodbye in the shadowy hall.

"Don't look like that," Jake said softly. "We'll see each other every day at the hospital."

Heather tried to smile. "I'm just worried about your back, sleeping on that big old lumpy couch of Derek's."

He grinned. "I've slept on worse. And I'll be leaving for Baltimore in August, anyway. It's only for a few weeks."

"Jake, I'm so sorry—" Heather started.

He touched her cheek gently. It was the briefest, barest touch, like a soft breeze against her skin.

"It's best," he said.

He turned and walked down the hall. He opened the door and slipped out, closing it softly behind him.

Heather slumped against the wall. Jake was right. She probably saw more of him at the hospital than she did at home. And they were still friends.

So why did she feel so alone?

A week later, Sherri called Corinne to go over the final details of their trips to Atlanta for the wedding.

"Okay, cool," Sherri said finally in approval. "If I book that evening flight, we'll arrive only ten minutes apart. That will make it easier for Heather. She seemed kind of stressed the last time we talked."

"I noticed that, too," Corinne agreed.

"Of course, that was over a week ago," Sherri admitted. "It's crunch time at work for me. Sometimes I wonder why I was crazy enough to turn down that Atlanta job."

"Hmmm," Corinne said. "Maybe because when push came to shove, you didn't want to drag Marc away from his family and a job he loves, even though he insisted it was okay?"

Sherri laughed. "Yeah, that must have been it. And my promotion helped. I just wish it hadn't come with a heavier work load. So when did you talk to Heather?"

Corinne scrunched a pillow against her neck and leaned back against the couch. Her cat Tiffin jumped up and nestled on her lap. "Just a few nights ago," she said. "If you think she sounded stressed a couple weeks ago, you should catch her now."

"I remember the drill," Sherri said, laughing. "I hit the panic button at least once a day before my wedding."

"I hear you," Corinne agreed. "And with Heather, it seems worse. You know how decisive she is? Well, she's let her future mother-in-law take complete charge of this wedding. It's scary. She's getting married in a huge church in a big elaborate gown. And did she tell you about the house?"

"Not Heather's style," Sherri agreed soberly. "But Corinne, you remember what it was like. Between trying to please yourself and your two families, you get so confused you can't remember what you liked in the first place."

"I know," Corinne said thoughtfully as she stroked the cat. "It wouldn't worry me so much except . . ."

"Except?" Sherri prodded.

"Well, you know that nice roommate she has, Jake Deveraux?"

"Dr. Dreamboat? Sure."

"Well, Reggie wanted her to kick him out. He said it didn't look right."

"He did?" Sherri asked, surprised. "Did she?"

"Nooo," Corinne said. "But he moved out anyway. Reggie got his way." She sighed. "I don't want to say anything against Reggie. I mean, I wouldn't be crazy about Jeff having a female roommate."

"Wouldn't that cozy cottage get a little crowded?" Sherri teased.

"I don't mean *now,* wise guy," Corinne said wryly. "Before the wedding. Tell me more about Reggie."

"I don't know him very well," Sherri said. "But he seemed really nice. You know Heather wouldn't hook up with someone who wasn't a good guy. And he's the handsomest man I think I've ever seen in my life. Except for Marc, of course," Sherri added hastily.

"I guess Reggie *does* have a point," Corinne said doubtfully. "But I still think Heather is acting kind of . . . well, wishy-washy."

"Wishy-washy? Heather?" Sherri hooted. "I never thought I'd hear those two things in the same sentence. But then again, for most of the time before my wedding I was pure tapioca."

"And I was a howling shrew," Corinne giggled. "Poor Jeff."

"And we made it through," Sherri said confidently.

"All the way to wedded bliss," Corinne agreed.

"Here's what I think we should do," Sherri said in her usual crisp, decisive style. "We'll make an effort to keep in touch even more often with Heather. Remind her of what weddings are all about. Love. We know she loves Reggie."

"So we keep her on track," Corinne agreed. "Remind her of how lucky she is to have found such a great guy.

And how all those things that seem so important just melt away on your wedding day.''

"Exactly," Sherri declared. "Pretty soon she'll be living in the upper fabusphere. Until then, we'll make sure our perfect girlfriend sails through her perfect wedding like a pro!''

Ten

 Heather stood on the lawn facing the large, gracious Southern home with white columns and a wide front porch. It was beautiful, no question. She could definitely picture it on the cover of a magazine devoted to genteel Southern living.

Maybe that was the problem. She'd never picked up one of those magazines in her life. Because when it came to actually *sitting* on that porch, she couldn't picture it. She couldn't imagine herself living here.

"Isn't it perfect?" Reggie asked.

"It's beautiful," Heather admitted.

"Mama has perfect taste," Reggie said, his eyes roaming over the exterior.

"I'm aware of that," Heather said dryly. "After all, she's planned our wedding."

"And she's done a great job, hasn't she?" Reggie beamed.

Heather nodded. Yes, Ruby had done a great job. Over the past weeks, every detail had fallen into place. The food would be exquisite. The band would play a selection of contemporary music and old dance favorites. The flowers would match the moonlight-pale shades of the bridesmaids' dresses. The champagne would be French, the bride's shoes Italian, and there would be Russian caviar sprinkled over the tiny new potatoes.

And Heather hadn't picked any of it. Oh, she'd been *consulted.* She'd been asked her opinion. But it was perfectly clear that Ruby was in charge.

And now, she'd found Heather a house. They wouldn't close until after the honeymoon. But Heather was expected to approve, and the sale would go forward. Heather had no doubt of that.

And if everything Ruby picks is so beautiful, so exquisite, aren't you selfish to complain?

Reggie squeezed her hand. "Come on. I can't wait to show you the inside. You'll flip."

With her hand securely in his, Reggie led Heather through the house. Their footsteps clicked on the polished hardwood floors. Their voices echoed in the high-ceilinged rooms.

It was grand. It was beautiful. It was like a dream.

I don't want it, Heather thought with a sense of despair that seemed to expand to fill every empty room.

Four bedrooms. A living room she could have fit her entire apartment in. A study, a front parlor, an enclosed back porch, a second-floor veranda. A laundry room, an eat-in kitchen, a dining room, a master bedroom with a bathroom centered around a huge marble jaccuzi that would have put her childhood kiddie pool to shame.

It all spelled one thing to Heather: *Monster Headache.*

"It's so big, Reggie," Heather said tentatively as they stopped in the middle of the living room to admire the Corinthian columns.

Reggie looked around in satisfaction. "Two more rooms than Geoffrey has."

"How am I going to clean it?" Heather asked doubtfully.

Reggie let out a ringing laugh. He swept her up in a hug. "You'll have help, silly," he told her fondly. "Do you think I want my wife scrubbing floors?"

"But all these rooms," Heather continued tentatively. "We'll have to fill them with . . . stuff."

Heather pictured filling the rooms. The thought made

her feel as though she were suffocating. She saw a house just like the Tylers'. Antiques, paintings, bedding, linens, tables, chairs, entertainment systems, porch furniture, pool furniture . . .

"Don't worry, you'll have help," Reggie reassured her. "*We'll* have help," he said quickly, as Heather gave him a wry look. "I'm a part of this, too, absolutely."

"I'm not afraid of the work," Heather told him. "I'm afraid of the *house*." She waved a hand. "It has so many . . . implications."

A hurt look came over Reggie's face. "You don't like it."

"It's beautiful," Heather said slowly. "But it seems like a place to *aspire* to. Not one to get right out of college."

Relieved, Reggie kissed the tip of her nose. "You're so cute. I bet it will only take you a month before you feel right at home. You're going to love this house."

Heather sighed. Reggie had grown up with luxury. He just didn't understand. Not that many people would. Some of her friends from school and work would be incredulous. She could hear them in her head.

Are you crazy? You don't want to live with a gorgeous husband in a big house with a BMW in the garage? Well, sign me up, girl.

The clatter of high heels in the front foyer reached them. Heather heard a high giggle that was beginning to sound irritatingly familiar.

"Come out, come out, wherever you are!" Adrienne sang. Another giggle sailed toward them.

"Can't we hide?" Heather whispered. "After all, there are what—fourteen closets?"

Reggie shot her a disapproving look just as Adrienne popped her head around the corner. "There you are!"

Yolanda tripped after her in high-heeled sandals. The two girls looked summery and fresh in their bare, bright print dresses.

"I hope you don't mind that we crashed your party,"

64

Adrienne said, strolling toward them. "Mama wants Yolanda's opinion on Reggie's new house. She knows all about these big old barns."

Yolanda smiled at Reggie. "I hope you don't mind."

"Mind?" Reggie said. "We're delighted."

"Delighted," Heather said.

"Heather was just saying how intimidated she was," Reggie went on. "She's got all these rooms to fill, and she's scared to death."

"I didn't really say that—" Heather started, but Yolanda broke in.

"Really?" she said, her brown eyes widening. "I'd be like a racehorse at the starting gate."

Heather saw Reggie give an appreciative glance at Yolanda's slender legs. "Now that's what I like to hear," he said.

She wanted to kick him. But instead, Heather touched his sleeve gently. "Reggie, I really should be getting back to work."

Frowning, he looked at his watch. "I thought you didn't have to be back until two. It's only one-fifteen."

Heather forced a smile. "Is that all? I thought it was later."

Adrienne looked impatient. "Are you going to show us the house or not, Reggie?"

"Absolutely," Reggie said promptly. "I have to find out Yolanda's opinion. Because we're not making a decision about the house until I know that she approves." He gave her a teasing wink.

Yolanda giggled. "I warn you, I have strict standards."

"Girl, you're scaring me now," Reggie kidded lazily.

Heather couldn't believe it. He was *flirting* with another girl, right in front of her! Fuming, she followed the two girls and Reggie out of the living room.

For the second time, Heather walked through room after room of the big house. She kept silent while Yolanda pointed out architectural details and gushed over the high ceilings and the bathroom fixtures and the "Palladian feel" of the upper gallery.

No one noticed that Heather didn't say a word. She could have floated out of the wide windows, and Reggie wouldn't have noticed. Yolanda kept on talking about "his" house and "his" period details as if she didn't even exist!

Heather hung back. With a sense of gloom, she noticed how the three were so alike in their beautiful clothes and expensive shoes. Heather felt like a hired laborer, clomping along in her loafers while Yolanda promenaded ahead of her in her delicate hot-pink sandals and her matching toenail polish.

The girl was examining the house as though *she* was going to buy it, Heather noted grumpily. Yolanda chirped to Reggie about wainscotting, alcoves, arches, and tongue-and-groove woodwork, whatever that was.

They came to rest on the back porch, where they stood looking out at the pool, landscaped to appear as if it were a tropical lagoon.

"So?" Reggie asked, his eyes twinkling. "Should I buy it?"

Yolanda pretended to hesitate. "Wellll . . ." Then she smiled. "Definitely."

Reggie grinned at Heather. "You see, sweetheart? We have a winner. Yolanda says so."

"I'm so glad," Heather said tonelessly.

Adrienne turned to her. "Heather, I had the most fabulous idea," she cooed in a honeyed voice. "I've been meaning to ask you. Can Yolanda be a bridesmaid? It would make it so much more fun for *me*."

Heather stared at Adrienne, speechless.

"And Mama thinks it's a great idea," Adrienne went on, as if that settled it. "After all, she's practically a sister. And it's always better to have an even number of bridesmaids. Mama said so."

Heather couldn't believe Adrienne's nerve. First of all, to ask if she would have a stranger who wasn't even family as a bridesmaid. Second, to ask *in front of* Yolanda! How could she possibly get out of this without being rude?

But Reggie solved her problem. He slipped his arm around Yolanda's bare shoulders.

"I think it's a fabulous idea," he said. "She's one of the family, Heather."

Heather's eyes burned at Reggie, and he dropped his arm casually.

"You don't mind, do you, Heather?" Adrienne asked impatiently. "What do you say?"

What can I say? Heather thought. *I'm trapped!*

Her teeth gritted in a strained smile. "Of course I don't mind, Adrienne," she said.

Eleven

 "Jealous? Not that again," Reggie groaned that evening. "You can't be serious."

Heather stood in the middle of her living room. She crossed her arms. "I'm as serious as the swine flu," she told him. "That girl was flirting with you, and you did nothing to stop it. You flirted right back, and I was standing right there! First of all, it was rude. And second of all, it's not the way I expect my husband to behave. It shows disrespect. I *won't* marry a man who treats me that way. And third of all, I *don't* want her as a bridesmaid!"

Heather finished, her hands clenched. Her eyes flashed sparks at Reggie. He sat on the couch staring down at his hands. He didn't speak. She waited calmly. She knew she was right. She wasn't going to stand for that behavior. Ever. No matter what excuses he made, or how he tried to charm her. No matter if he was defensive, or got angry back at her. She'd stand her ground.

But when Reggie looked up, his dark, soulful eyes were contrite. "You're right," he said quietly. "I apologize."

Heather stood, shocked and stiff, as he rose and came to her side. He didn't take her in his arms. He knew that she would only pull away.

"I'm so sorry, baby," he said, his eyes never leaving

hers. "All I can do is promise you that it will never happen again."

Heather was completely taken aback. She had prepared more arguments, ready for Reggie to tell her she was imagining things. She never expected him to apologize right off the bat!

Reggie sighed. "Look, honey. I can't lie to you. I've been flirting with girls all my life. It's as natural as brushing my teeth. And it's hard for me to just . . . stop doing what comes naturally." He gave her a rueful smile that almost disarmed her. But not quite.

She kept her arms crossed. "Well, you're going to have to find a way."

"I already have," he said. "I'll just stop. Because nothing is worth hurting you. Even a tiny bit. I can't forgive myself for hurting you. But can you find a way to forgive me?"

Heather hesitated. Despite the melting look in Reggie's liquid-dark eyes, she still wasn't ready to cave in.

"What about Yolanda?" she challenged. "That girl has her eye on you, Reggie."

"Maybe you're right," he conceded. "I just look at her as my little sister's friend. I've been trying to make her feel special."

"And maybe feed your own ego a little bit?" Heather pointed out, one eyebrow raised.

Reggie winced. "Ouch. Okay, maybe so. You know me too well, Heather. You never let me get away with anything. Can't you see that's why you're so good for me?"

His voice had turned low and hypnotic. He reached for her, but Heather stepped back.

"Reggie, this is serious," she said quietly. "You really hurt me and upset me."

"I'm so sorry," Reggie said, his eyes contrite. "I truly am, honey. I'll cool it with Yolanda. I'm going to forget that girl's name. And if you don't want her as a bridesmaid, you don't have to have her. I don't care. It's

69

just Adrienne, being pushy as usual. I can talk to her for you, if you want.''

Hesitantly, Heather shook her head. "Don't do that. I don't want Adrienne to hate me. She's going to be my sister-in-law. And I guess I don't want to hurt Yolanda's feelings, either.''

"Who?" Reggie asked, with a wicked grin.

"It's just that Yolanda is your type!" Heather burst out. "She's just like those girls you dated in college. She's petite and perfect. She knows about antiques, and she wears the right clothes, and she gets pedicures . . .''

He didn't laugh. She thought she might kill him if he did. Instead, Reggie took her hand, with her short, blunt nails and the ink stain on her forefinger. Slowly, he kissed every finger, keeping his liquid gaze on her.

"Don't you know that you're the only woman for me?" he asked, his voice rubbing against her like silk, like velvet. "Next to little puny girls like Yolanda, you're a goddess. You've got more style in this little finger right here than most girls have in their entire wardrobe. Because you're the real thing, Heather.''

Heather didn't say anything. She didn't have to. Reggie sensed her surrender the moment she made it. He brought her back to the couch and sat her on his lap. Then he brought her close to him for a long, delicious kiss.

Heather rubbed up against Reggie like a cat. He felt so smooth, so warm. And it felt so good not to fight. It felt so wonderful to lose herself in sweet, forgiving kisses.

"I'm going to make it up to you," Reggie murmured. "Tonight.''

She sighed, and her hand curled around his neck. But somewhere, a tiny, mocking part of her was disgusted with herself. She'd started out so strong, so confident, so sure of her position. Like a woman.

But she ended up curled in his lap. Like a little girl.

* * *

That night, Reggie cancelled the plans he'd made to go to the movies with the gang. Instead of a trendy, expensive restaurant, they drove to Heather's favorite Tex-Mex joint, José's.

They crunched on chips and salsa and ate enchiladas until they felt like bursting. Then they worked it off on the dance floor.

It was an evening just like they used to have. And she was smack back in love all over again.

Reggie insisted on making it an early night, since Heather had a heavy work load the next day. He paused to kiss her good night at her door.

"Just a warning. But if you invite me in tonight, I might not leave," he murmured against her lips.

"Then I'd better not," she said, smiling.

He touched a finger to her mouth. "Save my place, will you?"

She nodded, holding his gaze. "Always."

She watched him walk to his car with a smile on her face. That was the man she fell for. Considerate, sweet, funny. And she was sure now that she was the luckiest woman in the world.

Twelve

Heather's dreamy mood lasted until the next morning, when she got to the hospital. As she hurried down the hall, clipping her ID to her blouse, she saw Jake. He headed toward her, frowning, and she knew something was wrong.

"It's Algie Stokes," Jake told her. "He hemorrhaged last night. Bleeding from the G.I. tract. Dyspnea. Epistaxis—"

"Jake," Heather said gently. When Jake used medical terms she didn't understand, she'd usually tease him about being the Medical Machine. Today, she just wanted to know what was wrong.

He grimaced. "He came in with a severe nosebleed and bloody vomit. He had a reaction to the transfusion." He put a hand on Heather's arm. "He's been stabilized. He's such a strong kid—he's going to pull through. But his mother is a mess."

Startled, Heather looked at Jake. She'd never heard him volunteer information about a patient's family member before.

But he didn't notice her surprise. "I had a long talk with her this morning and explained that I have the best hopes for Algie. But nothing seemed to penetrate. Maybe you can get through. If anyone can, it's you, Heather."

Jake's worried gaze held hers. He touched her arm briefly. She nodded. "I'll do my best."

Heather hurried toward Algie's room. When she pushed open the door, his mother was holding the sleeping boy's hand, careful not to disturb his IV. Crystal turned toward her, her eyes glistening with tears.

"Oh, Heather," she cried softly. "I'm so glad you're here."

Heather crossed the room and placed a hand on Crystal's shoulder. She looked down at Algie. Her heart rose in her throat. The boy looked so fragile under the sheet. The thick, curling eyelashes she teased him about made shadows on his thin cheeks.

"Dr. Deveraux says he's going to be fine," Heather said, trying to sound firm and positive.

"I know. He's a good doctor." Crystal's hand stroked her son's slight fingers. "Oh, Heather. Last night—he couldn't stop bleeding, and there was nothing I could do. I couldn't stand to see my baby die!"

A sob broke loose from Crystal. Heather crouched down to face her. "Listen to me, Crystal," she said. Her voice was soft but firm. "He's not going to die. He's *not*. And you *did* do something. You brought him here. You recognized that something was very wrong. You acted quickly. You did everything right."

Crystal nodded through her tears. "That's what Dr. Deveraux said."

"Well, listen to him." Heather gave a tiny smile. "You should know by now that Dr. Deveraux doesn't say anything he doesn't mean."

"He doesn't say much at all, that man," Crystal said, with a hint of a smile in response. "But what he *does* say, I believe."

"Then believe him now. Algie will pull through. He has the heart of a lion, Crystal. Believe in your boy. Never stop believing."

Crystal's round, pretty face cleared. "Yes," she said. She straightened in her chair and her bright, dark eyes moved back to Algie. "Yes, I believe in my baby."

Heather pulled a chair over to sit next to Crystal. "Now, what about you? What about your job?"

"That's the other thing, Heather," Crystal said, turning a bleak gaze on her. "I called my boss this morning. He said he's real sorry about Algie. But if I take any more days off, he's going to let me go!" Fresh tears formed in Crystal's eyes. "We'll lose our insurance, Heather. Can you help me?"

For the rest of that long, exhausting day, Heather never stopped moving. First, she questioned Crystal closely about her job responsibilities. She placed a cup of steaming coffee and a sandwich in her hand and told her not to worry.

Then, she tracked down a member of the hospital board who owned a chain of electronic stores. Using all her powers of persuasion, Heather outlined the problem and asked for the loan of a laptop computer, modem, and even a cellular phone so that Crystal wouldn't have to pay hospital rates on Algie's room phone. When the executive agreed, she wanted to sing with joy. But she had to contact Crystal's employer.

That was the harder pitch. But Heather kept pushing. She pointed out that Crystal's job duties didn't require her presence in the office. She could easily telecommute for the short term. She outlined all the ways Crystal had been helpful to the firm, and what a valuable employee she was. Finally, she appealed to the boss's heart. What if *his* young son was lying in the hospital?

"All right, all right," the employer finally said. "You convinced me. She can set up a modem and telecommute. As long as she keeps track of shipments and keeps in touch by phone, it's okay." His voice lowered. "And how is the boy doing?"

"He's going to be all right," Heather answered. "And I want you to know that you'll have a great deal to do with his recovery. You could have saved a life today."

"I never looked at it that way," the employer said, pleased.

Heather hung up, pleased herself. A disaster had been avoided. A doctor had possessed the broadsight to see that a patient's problem extended beyond his diagnosis. A benefactor had found it in his heart to make a small loan of equipment. And an employer focused on business had stretched the rules of the office to accommodate an employee in need.

She swung around in her chair. Her plan had certainly been unorthodox. "But hey, it worked," she said under her breath.

She spent another half-hour with Crystal, explaining how her idea would work, and teasing Algie about getting out of the hospital fast enough to be the ring bearer at her wedding that weekend.

She was flying high as she left the Stokes, consulting her clipboard to find out which duty to accomplish next.

A short woman in black-framed glasses saw her heading down the hall. "Heather! There you are. Matanzas wants to see you, stat."

"What for, Dee?" Heather asked, tucking a pen in her pocket. Ms. Matanzas was her boss.

"Don't know. Hey, we heard about the Stokes case. Good going, girl." Dee grinned.

"Thanks." Heather hurried toward Ms. Matanzas's office. Maybe her boss had also heard about Heather's solution and wanted to congratulate her.

But as it turned out, her boss hadn't requested a meeting to congratulate her. She had asked to see Heather in order to fire her.

Ms. Matanzas looked at her sorrowfully. "This is the hardest thing I've had to do here," she said. "And in an age of budget cuts, that's saying something. But the money didn't come through, Heather. What can I say? We need you desperately. You've done an amazing job here. But we don't have the funds to hire you, even at a tiny salary."

Heather swallowed. "Thank you for trying."

"Sometimes, this job stinks," Ms. Matanzas said. She stood and offered her hand. "I'm sure you'll do brilliant things, Heather."

Heather shook it. "Thank you." She couldn't think of anything else to say.

"We'll miss you," Ms. Matanzas said, before Heather closed the door.

A lump in her throat, Heather hurried toward the phone in the lounge. She needed to hear Reggie's soothing voice telling her everything would be okay.

Reggie's voice oozed sympathy. "Oh, honey, that's terrible," he told her. "I can't believe these people. Don't they know a good thing when they see it?"

"It's not their fault," Heather said. "They don't have the funds for this kind of care."

"Well, it's stupid." Reggie sighed. "But at least you're getting married in two days. You won't have time to take a breath, let alone concentrate on a job. Sherri and Corinne are flying in tonight—they'll cheer you up."

"But Reggie—"

"And you'll get used to not working, sweetie," he said with a chuckle. "Listen, I've got to run. I don't like to leave you like this, but I've got a meeting. I'll take you out to dinner tonight, okay?"

Dinner out was Reggie's solution for everything, Heather thought with a sigh. "Okay. You go ahead to your meeting. I have to find Jake and tell him the news anyway."

When she tracked him down in the hospital garden, Jake was furious. He flung his half-eaten sandwich into the trash.

"This is outrageous," he said. "It's bad for you, Heather, but it's worse for the hospital. You made a *difference*. It's typical of the micromanage approach.

They don't realize how much money they *save* having you help these people."

"They should," Heather said wryly. "I wrote it all in my report requesting a full-time position."

"You really made a difference to patients," Jake said. "And me."

"You?"

Jake took her hand. "You taught me something, Heather. As an intern, you're under so much pressure. All you think about is diagnosis and treatment. All you look at are clogged blood vessels and diseased organs. Now I look at *people*. I look at families, not just patients." His fingers twined through hers and squeezed gently. "When I start my own practice, I'll be a different kind of doctor. Because of you."

Heather looked up into his face. The sun lit his amber eyes, like a ray of golden light through a honeycomb. His face was tight, intense, and she felt his strong fingers gripping hers. She felt lightheaded, and she remembered that she had skipped lunch. Her heart was definitely tripping a little too fast.

But had she ever really noticed how Jake's eyes glowed? How his skin had a burnished coppery look in summer?

How soft his mouth looked . . .

Heather swallowed. "Speaking of your practice, there's something I've been meaning to ask you for ages," she chattered nervously. "Why is it called a medical *practice,* anyway? Don't you think they would pick a more *confident* word?"

Jake grinned. His grip didn't loosen on her hand. "Don't change the subject. Heather, when I look at you, I see humor and grit and beauty and strength, all of it woven together. And I . . ."

Jake stopped. "Heather—"

He stopped again.

Lunch! Heather thought desperately. Or the lack

thereof. That was why she was feeling this way. Slightly dizzy. Slightly off balance.

"I need an enchilada," she blurted. "I forgot to have lunch."

"Shame on you," a familiar voice boomed.

Heather smothered a gasp. Her glowering fiancé stood at the head of the walkway while she held hands with Jake!

Thirteen

 Jake dropped her hand. She felt her face flush as Reggie strode toward them.

"How many times have I told you not to skip lunch?" Reggie scolded her as he reached her side. "You're going to waste away, sweetheart."

The bright red flowers behind Reggie's head looked fuzzy to Heather as he bent forward and slipped an arm around her.

"You need to be taken care of," he said. "That's why I cancelled my meeting and came straight here. I'm sorry about the job, honey. But don't let it worry you anymore. I'm going to make it all better. Jake, you'll have to excuse us. I've got to take care of my baby here."

Heather looked at Jake. She wanted to finish their conversation. It was so unusual for Jake to open up like that. What was it he was beginning to say?

But she knew it was hopeless. Reggie was ready to sweep her away, and Jake wouldn't even look her in the eye. He muttered a goodbye as Reggie took her by the arm and guided her out of the garden.

She was still dazed. Still shaky. She still felt as though the world was spinning just a little too fast for comfort.

Food, Heather told herself.

Protein . . . energy. I really need that enchilada. Then I'll be okay. Really.

Reggie was silent as they walked to the parking lot. Heather waited nervously for him to bring up that he'd seen Jake holding her hand. She could explain everything, of course. But Reggie didn't say a word about Jake.

"Why don't we grab something light?" he suggested as he hit the alarm button to unlock the BMW. "Sherri and Corinne are arriving in a few hours. We might want to go out with them for a bite later." He swung open the passenger door and waited for her to enter.

"Sounds good." Heather slid into the buttery interior of Reggie's BMW. As she settled back, something hard stuck into her back. While Reggie closed her door and moved around to the driver's side, she twisted in her seat. Probing into the crack of the seat, she withdrew a lipstick case just as Reggie sank into his seat.

The smile on his face faded when he saw what Heather was holding up and the accusing look in her eyes.

"Now, hold on," he said quickly. "Don't explode. Think about it. That lipstick has probably been rolling around in the car for ages."

"It wasn't rolling around," Heather said tightly. "It was in stuck in the seat. And it wasn't there last night. At least," she added, "when you dropped me off. Why did you drop me off so early, anyway? Did you go home afterward, Reggie?"

"Of course I went home!" Reggie said, annoyed. "I can't believe this. That lipstick could have been stuck in the seat for *months*. It's probably some old girlfriend I can't even remember the name of."

A sickening feeling crept into Heather's stomach as she tried to reason it out. She wanted to believe Reggie. Unfortunately, his explanation didn't make sense.

"Funny," she said, trying to hold back the pain. "It doesn't look grimy or dusty. Plus you just got this car detailed a week ago. They would have found it, don't you think? And if you're at a loss for the *name*, I can supply it. You haven't forgotten Yolanda, have you?''

"Yolanda! Not that again!''

"It's bad enough I have to have Dumbo for a brides-maid,'' Heather said furiously. "Now she's trying to steal my man right under my nose!''

"There's no call to insult the girl, Heather,'' Reggie said icily. "She's not stupid.''

"I'm not talking about her brains, I'm talking about her *ears*,'' Heather snarled. "That girl better be careful. She could take off in a high wind.''

"I don't believe this,'' Reggie said, slapping the steering wheel with the heel of his hand. "I'm seeing a whole ugly side of you I didn't know was there.''

"Me?'' Heather stared at him incredulously. She held up the lipstick. "It's not about me. *You're* the one who's cheating on me and *lying* about it!''

"I'm telling you, I'm not cheating!'' Reggie cried.

His protest was so sincere that Heather felt her resolve falter. Could somebody look so innocent and be guilty?

He frowned. "Wait a second. That lipstick must be Adrienne's. Of course—that's it! I gave her a ride to the club this morning. Her car wouldn't start.'' He shook his head sorrowfully. "I can't believe you jumped to conclusions like that. Don't you trust me at all?''

Heather bit her lip. She'd never considered that Reggie's sister had been in the car. "Maybe I *did* overreact. I'm sorry.'' She sighed. "I guess I'm stressed from the day I just had, Reggie. Of course I trust you.''

His face relaxed in a grin. He patted her knee. "Good. I'm glad that's settled. Now, let's eat. You definitely have some kind of low-blood-sugar thing going on. Dumbo!'' He chuckled under his breath.

Reggie started the car and pulled out into Atlanta's busy downtown streets. For the next few minutes, he concentrated on wrestling with rush-hour traffic.

While Reggie honked his horn and tried to make a left turn before the light turned red, Heather unscrewed the lipstick. It was a bright apricot shade. Definitely not a shade Heather would ever consider. She tried to go for a more natural look.

Tossing the hated tube of lipstick into her bag, she thought about returning it to Reggie's sister. There was just one problem with that. Adrienne wore earth tones. She wouldn't be caught dead in apricot.

But Heather remembered seeing this shade on someone else. Someone as flashy and flirty as the orange lipstick itself.

Yes, she'd seen a glistening apricot glaze on Yolanda's pouty lips.

Fourteen

 When Reggie and Heather reached the country club, the gang had already assembled. While Heather ate her salad, she watched Yolanda, who was sitting at the opposite end of the table with Adrienne. The girl didn't look at Reggie once.

But was that a *good* sign, or a bad one?

Yolanda was wearing pink lipstick tonight. Was that because she'd lost her apricot one?

Adrienne was wearing her usual earth tone—a muted shade of copper. But if Reggie was telling the truth, Adrienne could have borrowed Yolanda's lipstick. Maybe she'd wanted to try a different shade? Maybe they'd been exchanging makeup, the way girls often do. When Heather had lived near Corinne, they'd shared and borrowed clothes and accessories all the time—though Corinne's tastes definitely ran more casual than Heather's.

There was one other point supporting Reggie. When they pulled in, Heather didn't see Adrienne's red Miata in the parking lot. Was that because Adrienne had arrived in Yolanda's car—or because her car really was in the shop?

Heather speared her tomato deftly with her fork. *Keep cool, girl,* she told herself. If she couldn't trust her fiancé, how could she trust her husband? She had to have faith in the man she loved.

Heather gave a small sigh. She couldn't wait to leave for the airport to greet Sherri and Corinne. Once her friends were by her side, she knew she'd be okay. Between Sherri's enthusiasm and Corinne's sweet nature, she knew she could get her head on straight—and start looking forward to her wedding again.

A flying red cannonball hit Heather broadside. Sherri was never one to hold back her emotions. She flung her arms out, managing to squeeze Corinne and Heather together in her wide embrace.

"Together again!" she crowed, her red curls bouncing as she jumped excitedly.

Corinne and Jeff's plane had touched down first. Heather had a few quiet minutes to introduce them to Reggie before Sherri's flight landed. Sherri had been the first one off the plane. She'd probably bribed the flight attendant, Heather thought, grinning at her friend.

"I'm so glad to see you guys," Heather told them fervently.

Sherri put out her hand. Heather covered it with her own. Corinne followed. They stacked hands, making their familiar tower of power.

"Friends forever," they said together.

"Through thick and thin," Heather added.

Then, they burst out laughing. When the three girls turned, they saw their men standing in a row. Jeff and Marc were gazing fondly at them, smiling. Reggie was looking at his watch.

Reggie's suggestion that they hit the fifties style, all-night diner was met with enthusiastic approval.

"I don't know why flying always makes me ravenous," Sherri said, perusing the menu.

"Maybe it's the food," Marc suggested. "That meat bore *some* resemblance to chicken, but I didn't take any chances."

Corinne put down her menu and raked her honey-blond bangs out of her eyes. "I'm going to try the five-alarm chili with cheese and onions on top."

Jeff shuddered. "If you have nightmares, don't wake me up."

"Who's going to comfort me?" Corinne asked, her eyes twinkling. "I left my cats at home."

Jeff groaned. "I guess that means me."

But he said it with affection, and Heather saw him squeeze her hand.

Throughout the meal, Heather was quiet, watching her friends. She noticed how, when Sherri spilled her soda in her excitement, Marc just handed her a napkin, but didn't criticize her. She saw how Jeff's gaze rested fondly on Corinne's face as she told a story. She smiled as Marc laughed helplessly at one of Sherri's zany jokes. She noted how, without a word, Jeff pushed his french fries closer to Corinne to share.

Heather looked down at her own food. She'd ordered her favorite indulgence, a cheeseburger platter. She'd asked for extra pickles, but instead, the platter had arrived with no pickle at all.

Heather scanned the crowded diner for their waitress. "What is it, honey?" Reggie asked her.

"I didn't get my pickles," she said.

"I'll tell the waitress." But after a moment of trying fruitlessly to signal her, Reggie returned his attention to his own food and a story he was telling about his promotion he was gunning for at work. He wanted a title equal to his brother's within three months after the wedding.

Heather squirted mustard and ketchup on her burger. She liked to cut up the pickles in thin slices and garnish the burger, but she could do without.

She ate slowly, watching Reggie tell her friends about the family business. She knew that Sherri and Corinne liked him. After all, who could resist Reggie's charm?

Reggie ate his own cheeseburger while he joked with Corinne about her pet referral service and her studies.

He cleared his plate while he asked Sherri's advice about the Tyler Corporation's offices. And he ate his pickle. All of it. Heather was thoughtful as she watched him chomp away.

The waitress reappeared long enough to deposit the check. Reggie reached for it before anyone could move.

"My treat," he said. "I insist. You guys flew all the way here just for Heather."

"I'd argue with the man, but I don't think it would do any good," Marc said.

Reggie stood. "It wouldn't," he said, flashing his handsome grin. He made his way to the cash register.

Immediately, Sherri and Corinne turned to Heather.

"He looks like a movie star," Corinne said. "But you can tell he isn't vain."

"We told you that you'd find the perfect man," Sherri teased. "Even if he *hasn't* won the Nobel Prize."

"Yet," Corinne put in, smiling.

"I just love his big brown eyes, don't you, Jeff?" Marc said mockingly.

"It's those big strong arms that get to *me*," Jeff answered, stone-faced.

Giggling, Sherri and Corinne swatted their husbands.

"Shut up, you guys," Sherri said. "Admit it. Heather has found her perfect match. Just like we did."

"Now *that* I'd agree with," Marc said, giving Sherri an affectionate look.

But he didn't offer me his pickle! Heather wanted to wail.

She bit her lower lip, holding back the words. She knew it would just sound childish. Crazy. Maybe she *was* crazy. She was focusing on a pickle, for heaven's sake. Talk about obsessing over minor details!

You're just tired and upset about losing your job, she told herself. She could worry about that later. For now, it was time to enjoy her best friends in the world—for the brief time that they'd be together. Sherri and Corinne were here. They'd given their seal of approval on Reggie. And Reggie was flashing her that grin that could melt the paint off a battleship.

All was right with the world.

Fifteen

The next day, Heather, Corinne, and Sherri headed for the bridal shop. The girls were scheduled to try on their bridesmaid's dresses, and Heather would have her final fitting.

On the drive over, Corinne and Sherri were full of questions about the wedding. They demanded that Heather drive them by the house Reggie wanted to buy, and oohed and ahhed over how beautiful it was.

"I can see where Marc and I will be spending our vacations," Sherri said.

"Do you take pets?" Corinne joked.

Heather tried to laugh with the two girls, but it stuck in her throat. She still couldn't picture living in that huge house with Reggie.

Corinne was the one to notice Heather's mood as Heather swung the car out of the grand driveway and turned toward downtown Atlanta.

"Are you okay, Heather?" Corinne asked. "You seem kind of down."

Corinne and Sherri had talked so much about how "perfect" Heather's life was going to be that she couldn't bear to burst their bubble. She was embarrassed to tell Corinne, who struggled with finances, or Sherri, who approved of Ruby's taste, that she didn't know if she wanted the glittering future spread out before her.

"I guess it's my job," she said finally. "I was so disappointed that it didn't work out."

"I know you loved working there," Sherri agreed. "And I *know* they need you. It really stinks."

Heather pulled into the parking lot of the bridal boutique. She turned off the car and shrugged. "I guess things would have been different if I'd stayed, anyway. Jake's moving to Baltimore in a few weeks." She turned to her friends. "I'm going to miss him so much. He's such an amazing doctor. Even when he's totally stressed and busy, he takes time with each patient. Everyone says he's a brilliant diagnostician. But he has compassion along with it. And he can be so *funny*. He really makes me laugh."

"He sounds like one in a million," Corinne said.

"He is," Heather said fervently.

When they got inside the shop, Heather was led off to be buttoned into her gown. Sherri turned to Corinne.

"Did you catch that testimonial?" she asked in a low voice.

Corinne nodded. "He's a good friend of Heather's."

Sherri shook her head thoughtfully. "She never talks about Reggie that way. Do you think something's wrong?"

"I don't think so," Corinne answered softly. "But last night at the diner, she seemed kind of . . . off."

Sherri nodded. "I think there still could be mother-in-law problems. I mean, who would have imagined Heather having a big society wedding? And can you picture her living in that huge house? It's beautiful, but is it Heather? She's not a 'burb type, you know?"

"But she loves him," Corinne said. "She'll find a way to fit into his life."

Just then, two attractive African-American girls swept into the shop. They were dressed similarly in beautifully cut linen dresses.

"One of you *has* to be Reggie's sister," Sherri said,

smiling. "You're both too gorgeous to be ordinary mortals."

Adrienne smiled. "Guilty. I'm Adrienne Tyler, and this is my friend Yolanda. She's a bridesmaid, too."

Sherri and Corinne introduced themselves. They had just finished shaking hands when Heather popped out of the dressing room in the gown. All conversation stopped.

"Wow," Corinne breathed.

"You look beautiful," Sherri said tearily.

"My mother picked out the gown," Adrienne said.

Heather's face fell when she saw Adrienne and Yolanda. She quickly tried to cover by asking if they'd met Sherri and Corinne. But Sherri's green eyes narrowed.

Something was *definitely* off.

Corinne and Sherri circled around Heather, admiring the gown.

"At least *one* of us is going to have a six-foot train," Sherri said.

"Look at those covered buttons. Aren't they exquisite?" Corinne pointed out.

"You should definitely have Adrienne do your makeup, Heather," Yolanda advised. "She's a wizard."

"I don't wear much makeup," Heather said, bending over to fuss with her train.

"I know," Yolanda said. "But on your wedding day, you want to look glamorous."

Heather gave Yolanda a cool look. "Reggie likes me to look natural."

Yolanda giggled. "Sure, men *say* that."

"You said that right," Adrienne agreed with a laugh. "I never met one who didn't like lipstick."

At the mention of lipstick, Heather seemed to flinch. *What is going* on? Sherri wondered.

Adrienne turned to Heather. "Oh, Heather," she drawled, "did I tell you my Miata broke down? I just got it back from the shop. These past two days, I thought I would die without my car. You know how much I love my Miata, girl. Thank goodness I had a kind brother to take me around.''

Sherri watched in amazement as Heather broke into a dazzling smile. You'd think Adrienne's car trouble was the best news in town.

''Sorry to hear that, Adrienne,'' Heather said happily.

The saleswoman popped out of the dressing room, her arms full of the delicate silk chiffon dresses Sherri and Corinne would wear. She beckoned to the girls, and they followed her into the dressing room.

As soon as the saleswoman had left them alone, Sherri turned to Corinne.

''Did you notice that strange vibe between Heather and Yolanda?'' she whispered.

Corinne was pulling her T-shirt over her head, and her voice was muffled. ''What vibe?''

''And why did Heather light up when Adrienne told her she'd had car trouble?'' Sherri wondered. ''It's very mysterious.''

Corinne began to wiggle out of her jeans. ''I didn't really notice,'' she confessed. ''Do you want to wear peach or this pale blue?''

''Peach. You look better in blue.'' Sherri sighed as she ran her hand down the drifting silk chiffon of her dress. ''All I can say is, I'm glad I don't have another best friend,'' she said decidedly. ''I just couldn't take the pressure of another wedding!''

Sixteen

 For weeks, Heather had been dreading the rehearsal dinner. She'd made reservations at her favorite French country restaurant. Since her parents would be paying for the meal, Heather had not cracked under Ruby's pressure to have it at a more exclusive spot.

But she worried. What if that *look* came over Ruby's face when she walked into the small, charming spot? What if no one had anything to say? What if her sister Talia finally got over her awe of the Tylers and shot one of her well-known stinging barbs when Ruby dropped the words "Palladian" or "beluga caviar"?

But Heather had wasted time worrying. Her parents' flight was grounded in Baltimore, where they'd gone first to pick up Talia and do more research. They wouldn't be able to fly in until the next morning.

"We'll have to cancel the rehearsal dinner," Heather told her mother over the phone. She sunk onto the sofa, feeling oddly relieved. "Don't worry about it, Mama. I'll call the restaurant owner right now."

"I'm sorry to disappoint you, baby," her mother said.

"Hey, it couldn't be helped," Heather told her. "Just focus your prayers on getting the weather cleared up before morning. I can't get married without you and Daddy!"

When Heather hung up, Sherri gave her a doubtful

look. "Your rehearsal dinner is cancelled and you're happy?" she asked, referring to the smile of relief on Heather's face. "What's wrong with this picture?"

Heather turned away to pour herself a cup of tea. "You know how it is when you're down to the wire," she said vaguely. "Any reprieve is welcome."

"Mmmm," Sherri said.

"I wish I'd missed *my* rehearsal dinner," Corinne said with a shudder. "I nearly ended up without a family *or* a fiancé."

"Well, cheer up, girls," Sherri joked. "We still have the rehearsal to get through."

With the pressure of the dinner off, Heather dressed happily for the rehearsal in a navy silk dress that Reggie had picked out for her. He had told her that now that she was out of school, it was time for a more sophisticated look. Heather had resented his interference a little bit, but she had to admit that the dress was flattering.

The three girls left for the church. Jeff and Marc had snagged tickets to a Braves game, and had promised to meet the girls later that evening at Heather's apartment.

"Wow," Corinne breathed as Heather parked in the church lot. "This place looks like a cathedral."

"Who are you, Princess Di?" Sherri asked.

"It's where *everyone* gets married in Atlanta, darling," Heather said airily, imitating Ruby.

They stood in the back of the church, staring down the long, long aisle and row after row of pews.

Sherri started to whistle, but she stopped when she remembered she was in church.

"But did you mention that everybody in Atlanta was here at the same *time?*" Sherri said in a hushed voice. Corinne giggled.

Heather barely heard them. She stood still, gazing at the knot of people waiting at the altar. The distinguished couple, Andrew and Ruby Tyler. Debutante Adrienne Tyler in a designer suit. Reggie's brother Geoffrey must have come straight from the office. He was wearing an Armani suit. Brianna wore a navy silk dress much like Heather's. The elegant group all seemed to have come from the same mold.

For a moment, Heather felt disoriented. *Who are these people?* she wondered. *They're not my people.*

But then Corinne touched her arm. "Earth to Heather," she said softly.

"We'd better get moving," Sherri said. "The Dragon Lady keeps looking at her watch."

Heather shook off the strange feeling. She started down the aisle to greet her new family.

Ruby frowned as they came up. "I thought Reggie would be with you."

"He told me he'd meet me here," Heather said. She looked at her watch. "He should be here soon."

"We'll just have to wait for him and Yolanda," Mr. Tyler said.

In the silence that followed, Heather's heart beat faster. Yolanda wasn't here, either.

It doesn't mean anything, she scolded herself. *It doesn't mean they're together. It just means that they're both late.*

"That Reggie." Ruby gave a small, nervous laugh. "My boy has never been able to get anywhere on time."

Andrew Tyler smiled reassuringly at Heather. "Maybe the first present you get your husband should be a new watch."

Everyone laughed a little too hard at this joke. Heather noticed Adrienne glance at the church door nervously.

Fifteen long, slow minutes ticked by. Even Sherri couldn't get a conversation going. Ruby's face slowly turned to stone. Heather could only sit in a pew, her foot jiggling nervously.

Finally, the minister cleared his throat. "I suggest we get started," he said. "I have another church function to get to. Why doesn't the best man stand in for the groom, just for this evening? I'm sure the groom won't mind."

"I'm sure he *will*," Geoffrey said with a smile at Heather. "But I'd be glad to."

Heather rose and went to Geoffrey's side. He smiled at her warmly. *Everyone is feeling sorry for me,* she thought shakily.

"Geoffrey, as best man, you'll be stepping back here," the minister directed. "Bridesmaids over here—"

Suddenly, the church door crashed open. Everyone swiveled and looked up the long aisle. Reggie hurried down it, followed by Yolanda, clattering behind him in her high-heeled pumps.

"Relax, everyone." Reggie's voice boomed in the empty church. "We're fine. Just a flat tire."

He moved up smoothly next to Heather. "I can take over from here, bro," he said to Geoffrey.

Heather shot Reggie a sidelong look. "It's a bad week for the Tyler cars," she remarked dryly. "First Adrienne's, then yours."

"What was that?" Ruby called from the first pew. "Did you say Adrienne's? I didn't hear about this. We just bought you that Miata six months ago!"

"It's nothing, Mama," Adrienne said quickly. "Just a dead battery. I left the radio on. I was afraid to tell you."

Heather watched Yolanda's face. She looked right at Reggie and smiled.

But was it a sign? Or just that Yolanda had an innocent crush, just the way Reggie said?

The minister cleared his throat again. "Well, now. We have the groom. So let's begin."

Heather took her place beside Reggie. Outwardly calm, inside her heart was burning.

Yes, the groom is right here next to me. But do I really have him?

Seventeen

After the rehearsal broke up, Heather shook hands with the minister, said goodbye to the Tylers, and started for the door. Corinne and Sherri hurried to follow.

Reggie caught up to her on the church steps. "Where are you running to? You know you're in better shape than I am," he said, smiling.

Sherri and Corinne looked from Reggie to Heather's stony face. "We'll wait for you at the car," Corinne said, and the two walked off.

Reggie put his arms around her. "Don't be getting chilly on me now," he said. "I know it looked bad in there. But it didn't mean anything."

"Why were you with Yolanda?" Heather asked.

"Because she called the house to ask Adrienne for a ride. Adrienne had already left, so I offered. That's all." He sighed. "Heather, we've had this problem before. I promised you I wouldn't flirt with other women in front of you, and I meant it."

"You promised not to flirt with other women *at all!*" Heather exploded angrily.

"That's what I meant," Reggie said soothingly. He tilted her chin so that she had to look at him directly. "Heather, I love you. Do you believe that?"

His gaze was so intense. How could a man look so sincere, so straight, and lie, right to her face? Reggie *couldn't* do that. Not her Reggie. She had to believe her man.

"I believe you," she said quietly. "It's just that—"

He leaned forward and kissed her. His lips lingered on hers. "You're my girl," he murmured in the silky, insinuating voice that always sent shivers down her spine. "And I'll see you tomorrow, heading down that aisle all dressed in white, looking so fine and beautiful, and I'll see my future. You've *made* my future, baby. And I know that it's right."

He kissed her again, his hands sliding over her back. "Good night now," he whispered. "You sleep tight. And remember that I love you."

"Good night," Heather said. She *wanted* to tell Reggie that she loved him, too. But she couldn't. She felt too confused.

He waited for a moment. But Heather just turned and hurried away.

When the girls reached Heather's apartment, Marc and Jeff had already returned from the baseball game. They'd also had just enough time to completely destroy Heather's kitchen.

Marc stood at the stove, his apron splattered with tomato sauce. "Spaghetti, sausage, salad, and my deluxe garlic bread. How does it sound?"

"Like heaven," Sherri said, kissing him.

"As long as we don't have to clean up," Corinne said, eyeing the pots in the sink.

Jeff grinned at Heather. "We wanted to make up for your missing your fancy rehearsal dinner. Pizza just didn't cut it."

"You guys are the best," Heather said, smiling at them.

"Well, we only pick the best," Corinne said, kissing her husband's cheek. "We'll do the dishes."

Seeing Corinne smile at Jeff, Heather felt a pang of guilt. She was marrying Reggie tomorrow. How could she have withheld love from him? How could she have not trusted him? People got flat tires all the time, didn't they?

Heather pressed her hands to her head. She felt as though she was losing her mind.

"You okay?" Corinne asked, her eyes worried.

"Just a headache," Heather said briefly. "I'll take some aspirin."

Marc and Jeff turned out to be terrific cooks. The pasta was spicy and delicious. The garlic bread was like heaven. But Heather could only pick at her food.

"I couldn't eat a thing the night before my wedding," Corinne said. "Of course, I was in the middle of a family trauma and had just blown off my dad." She grinned at Jeff. "It's amazing we made it to the church."

"I couldn't eat, either," Sherri said, forking up a huge mass of spaghetti. "Probably because Marc wasn't speaking to me."

"Hey, I thought *you* weren't speaking to *me*," Marc said. "Which in itself was a miracle. When Sherri's mad, the whole world knows it."

Heather knew they were trying to make her feel better. They were trying to let her know that plenty of people were nervous before they got married. Weddings could be filled with misunderstandings as well as joy.

She pushed her plate away. "Will you guys excuse me? I need to call Reggie."

"You're just trying to get out of the dishes," Sherri said with an exaggerated sigh.

"But we'll excuse you," Corinne said.

Heather took the remote phone into her bedroom and closed the door. Reggie was spending his last night as a bachelor at his parents' house. She dialed the Tylers' number, hoping he'd answer the phone.

Instead, she got Ruby. Reggie's mother sounded surprised to hear from her.

"I'm sorry, Heather, but Reggie is already asleep," Ruby told her.

Heather glanced at the clock. It was barely nine-thirty. Reggie was a night owl. How could he have gone to bed? Would Ruby lie to her? Her future mother-in-law *did* sound evasive.

"Now, Heather, you take a page from Reggie's book and go to bed yourself," Ruby said firmly. "You don't want to have puffy eyes tomorrow." Her voice softened. "Everything will be all right tomorrow, Heather. You're going to have a perfect wedding. I promise you that. Good night, dear."

Heather's head was buzzing as she hung up the phone. Was everyone lying to her—Reggie, Adrienne, and now, even Ruby?

Slowly, she headed back to the kitchen. Sherri and Corinne had started the dishes. Marc and Jeff were in the living room, watching TV.

"Feel better?" Corinne asked.

Heather sank into a kitchen chair. She began to shred a paper napkin. "He was already asleep," she said. "At least, that's what Ruby told me."

Sherri turned from the sink. "Wait a second, Heather. You can't think that something is really going on between Reggie and that waif. Have you checked out those ears of hers?"

In spite of her sore heart, Heather had to smile. "I'm so glad you said that."

"Do you really think he's fooling around on you?" Corinne asked, pressing the issue.

Slowly, Heather nodded. She gave up on shredding the napkin and tore it in half.

Sherri looked at Corinne. Corinne threw down the dishtowel, and Sherri turned off the running water. The two girls joined Heather at the kitchen table.

"Okay, girl," Corinne ordered. "Spill."

Heather took a deep breath. She told her friends of her doubts and suspicions. About Reggie dropping her off unusually early. About finding the lipstick. About

Adrienne's dead battery and Yolanda's secretive smiles and Reggie's denials.

It all came out. But it didn't come out very coherently. Heather felt as though she were babbling, but she couldn't seem to organize her thoughts. She jumped from the rehearsal to the lipstick to the timing of Adrienne telling her about her car trouble. Everything made sense in her head, but she was afraid it sounded confusing to her friends.

"Heather, I can understand your feelings," Corinne said slowly. "But everything could just *look* bad, you know? You don't have any proof that Reggie is cheating on you."

"Especially with that puny thing," Sherri snorted. "She just has a crush on him. You know how that appeals to a guy's ego."

"I'm sure he *is* sleeping right now," Corinne said gently. "Ruby wouldn't lie to you."

Heather dabbed at her nose with a piece of the napkin. "I don't know about that. But even if Reggie is telling the truth, there are other things."

"Like?" Sherri prompted.

"Like the pickle!" Heather burst out.

Sherri and Corinne exchanged glances. "The pickle," Corinne repeated.

"The night you guys arrived," Heather explained, "and we went to the diner, there was no pickle with my cheeseburger platter. Reggie *knows* how I like my cheeseburger. I put lots of ketchup and mustard on it and then slice the pickle on top."

"And?" Corinne said gently.

"He didn't even give me a *bite* of his. And Jeff gave you the rest of his french fries!" she wailed to Corinne. "How can I marry a man who won't share his pickle?"

Heather broke into sobs of anguish. Tears rolled down her face, and Sherri picked up the half-torn napkin and handed it to her.

"This is definitely night-before-the-wedding jitters,"

she assured Heather. "It happens even before *perfect* weddings."

"We both had it, and we recognize the signs," Corinne said soothingly. "Even though you've met your perfect match, you convince yourself that he's a rotten human being."

"I mean, Heather, get real," Sherri said. "You're getting hysterical about a *pickle!*"

"Reggie might not have noticed your lack of pickle," Corinne pointed out. "And even if he did, maybe he was too nervous about meeting us to remember to share it. Let me tell you, girlfriend, Jeff might share his french fries, but he's a fiend about his mint chocolate chip ice cream." Corinne giggled. "If you think I can even get in one little lick, you're crazy."

Sherri and Corinne laughed, but Heather's face changed. Instead of being creased with worry and misery, it became calm and composed. It was a new, strange Heather, without the warmth and humor that usually animated her pretty face. Sherri and Corinne stopped laughing.

"You guys must be right," Heather said in a strange, hollow voice. "I must be crazy to doubt Reggie. That's what he keeps telling me, too. That's what his sister tells me, and his mother tells me, so it has to be true. I *am* the one who's mean and suspicious. I must be to doubt a man who says he loves me so much. Who insists that he's innocent with so much sincerity."

"Heather—" Corinne started, but Heather interrupted.

"I've got to be *crazy* to turn away from such perfection," she went on, her voice escalating slightly. "I must be out of my *mind* to think of giving up the perfect life he can give me. I should probably be *committed* for even considering that he's any less than perfect. Because I always choose right, don't I? I'm the sensible one. I'm the cautious one." Heather stood up so abruptly that her kitchen chair slammed against the wall. "You're always telling me I'm perfect, so how could I be wrong? Right?''

"Heather, that's not what we—" Sherri began, but Heather was already moving toward the door.

She snatched her car keys from the counter. "I have to check on a patient. Don't wait up."

Heather ran out of the kitchen. A moment later, they heard the front door slam.

Sherri and Corinne sat in silence for a moment. Finally, Sherri spoke.

"We laughed at her, Corinne," she said in a low, meek voice. "We didn't listen to her. We just keep pushing her fears away, telling her that all her wedding jitters are just like ours were. But they're not, are they?"

"No," Corinne said worriedly. "They're not."

Sherri blew out a breath. "We just blew it, didn't we?"

Corinne nodded. "Big time. The question is, what are we going to do about it?"

Eighteen

 The night duty nurse looked up from a chart when Heather approached. Without asking, she knew who Heather had come to see.

"Algie is sleeping," she told her. "But you can look in on him."

"Thanks, Diane," Heather said. She walked softly down the hall and pushed open the door.

The room was lit by a shaded lamp. Algie slept peacefully in his bed. Heather tiptoed a little farther into the room. In the next bed, Crystal was sleeping. Her hand rested on a children's book in her lap. Gently, Heather removed it and placed it close by on the bedside table. She knew that Crystal read to Algie until he fell asleep.

Watching the two of them as their chests rose and fell, seemingly in unison, Heather felt moved. She could feel the powerful love in the room like a living presence. With a last silent prayer, she tiptoed out.

She'd gone halfway down the hallway before she stopped. Suddenly, she felt too tired to even take another step. Heather leaned against the cool tiled wall.

Soft footsteps came from behind her. Probably a nurse or doctor making evening rounds. Heather felt a hand on her shoulder. She turned, and it was Jake.

"He's much better," he said.

"I know. Oh, Jake." Heather sighed. "There's so

much sorrow in the world. Sometimes I just can't bear it.'' She gazed at him searchingly, her eyes brimming with tears. ''How do you do it?''

Jake hesitated, obviously thinking about her question. ''The day I stop feeling sorrow is the day I won't be a good doctor, Heather. In a funny way, I have to be glad to be feeling it. Sorrow can nourish us. Make us deeper. Stronger.'' One corner of his mouth lifted. ''At least, that's what I tell myself. Some nights, it doesn't seem to help.'' He patted her shoulder. ''Come on. Let's grab a cup of decaf.''

The lounge was empty, lit only by one lamp on a far table. Jake didn't bother to turn on the lights. He poured two cups of coffee and handed one to Heather.

''So,'' he said. ''What are you doing here on the night before your wedding?''

Heather twined her fingers around the plastic cup. ''Thinking, I guess.''

He took a sip. ''About what?''

''Marriage,'' Heather said. ''Love. Life.'' She shrugged and gave a little laugh. ''Just the small stuff.''

''Ah. And what conclusions have you reached?''

''No conclusions,'' Heather said. ''That's the problem. I just keep thinking about Reggie's vision of a good life. Is it the same as mine? In many ways, we're so different. But will that feed our marriage, or wear it down?''

Jake just sipped his coffee, watching her with his quiet, steady gaze.

''But the most important thing is, do I really trust him?'' Heather brooded, staring down at her coffee. ''I mean, trust him the way I should trust a husband. All the way, right down to the bottom.'' She raised her eyes to Jake's. ''The way I trust you,'' she said softly.

She saw Jake take a sharp, indrawn breath.

Heather looked down again. ''The thing is,'' she continued, ''I keep coming back to the same thing. I love him.''

Carefully, Jake put his coffee cup down on the table. "Then that's all that matters," he said. "Heather, you should be talking to Reggie about all this. Not me."

"You're right," Heather said. "And in the end, marriage is always a chance, isn't it?"

Jake nodded stiffly. "I guess."

His face seemed taut and strained. He looked so tired, Heather thought. He must be working around the clock, and here she was burdening him with her problems.

"You look beat," she said sympathetically. "Are you okay? Is it work?"

"Not really," Jake answered shortly. "I made a wrong decision a while ago. I'm trying to learn to live with it."

"About Johns Hopkins?" Heather asked. "Or something in your personal life—"

Jake stood up abruptly. "Tonight isn't the night to talk about it, Heather. You're right. I am tired."

Heather rose more slowly. "If you need to talk—"

"No." Jake sounded almost angry. "Go home. Get a good night's sleep. Tomorrow is your wedding day."

Still, Heather hesitated by his side. "Thank you, Jake," she said softly. "I don't know what I'd do without you. We'll be friends forever, won't we? No matter what?"

She put her hand on his sleeve. Jake gently removed it. Then, in a gesture so tender it broke her heart, he brought it against his heart and held it there.

"Of course we will," he said huskily. "Now get out of here."

Heather smiled and nodded. She headed for the door. As it swished shut behind her, she thought she heard him speak.

"And have a good life . . ."

But that would sound so final. She must have imagined it.

Nineteen

 From the moment Heather awakened on her wedding day, she didn't have time to sit down, let alone think. Her parents and Talia arrived early, their arms full of boxes of the pastries they'd brought from Baltimore's Little Italy.

There were hugs and kisses and warm greetings to Corinne, Sherri, and their husbands. There was packing to do for the honeymoon to Bermuda. There were showers to coordinate and stockings that suddenly went missing. There were trips to the airport to organize. Soon, her tall, handsome brothers arrived to cries of happiness and much laughter.

Through it all, the doorbell kept pealing. Heather went through her duties methodically. She slipped away to the beauty parlor with her mother and Talia to get her hair done. She found the something old, something new, something borrowed, and something blue. She did it all on autopilot, because she didn't have a moment to think.

She knew Sherri and Corinne were trying to get her alone. They probably wanted to apologize for last night. But Heather didn't have time.

It's better this way, she thought as her mother placed the headpiece on her head and stepped back, tears in her eyes.

When the limousine arrived, she was ready. Everything had been done, everyone had been picked up, everyone had been fed lunch, everyone was happy, everyone was excited, everyone was thrilled.

It was her wedding day.

Heather had never truly believed that all those pews could be filled with people. Her hands felt clammy as she surveyed the rows of summer hats and heard the murmur of expectant guests waiting for the star attraction: The Bride.

She saw Sherri and Corinne start toward her. Their faces were worried over the drifting panels of silk chiffon. Heather turned to her father.

"Dad? Could you do me a favor?"

"Anything," he told her. "A glass of water?"

"I need to see Reggie," Heather said in a low tone.

"See the groom? That's one thing I *can't* do," her father said jovially. "It's bad luck."

But after a glance at Heather's serious, set face, he nodded. "What do you want me to do?" he asked quietly.

Heather waited nervously in the small anteroom. It was a dim room with a small, stained-glass window. Faint rays of sunlight struggled to penetrate the thick glass. They succeeded in staining her white dress with patches of green and yellow.

The door creaked open. Reggie frowned when he saw her. He shut the door behind him and took two strides into the room.

"Heather, this is ridiculous—" he started.

"No," she said softly. "It's serious."

"It had better be," Reggie said, looking at his watch. "The ceremony is supposed to start in exactly four minutes, Heather. You know how my mother feels about time—"

"It's *my* wedding!" Heather snapped.

Reggie looked surprised. "Hey, there's no reason to get hysterical—"

"I'm not hysterical," Heather said in a measured tone. "What I want to do is talk to you. And if you'd stop worrying about your mother for one minute, we can get this over with."

Reggie gave an aggrieved sigh. "All right. What is it, Heather?"

But now that she had his attention, she didn't know where to start. But Reggie was right; the clock was ticking.

"First of all, I want to know how you really feel about my working full-time," she said. "If I get a job in social services, are you going to stand up to Ruby and support me?"

"Yes, of course I will," Reggie said. "Is that all this—"

"Second, where were you last night?" Heather rapped out. "I called after the rehearsal."

"I went to bed," Reggie said. He checked his watch. "Heather, come on."

"Were you out with Yolanda?"

"Of course I wasn't," Reggie said, exasperated. He looked at his watch again.

"Reggie, I intend to be married to one person for the rest of my life," Heather said. "I can only do that if I'm absolutely sure that the person I'm marrying is as committed to me as I am to him. As interested in being equal partners as I am. I need a man who has as much respect for me as I have for him. I want to know, right now, if you feel the same way."

"Of course I feel the same way," Reggie said impatiently. "I respect you. I'm interested in being equal partners. Whatever." He looked at his watch again. "Now I'd really better get back. People will talk!"

Reggie started toward the door. He paused with his hand on the knob and turned to look at her. "What's up with you?" he asked, his forehead creasing. "I know you love me. It's going to be a perfect day. Don't spoil it." Frowning, he walked out and closed the door.

Heather sat for a moment, breathing quietly. Then she stood up and smoothed her skirts. She adjusted her head-piece. She straightened her shoulders and made her way slowly to the back of the church.

This time, Sherri and Corinne were able to corner her.

"Heather, we need to talk, and we need to talk fast," Sherri said rapidly. "Now, don't try to avoid us, you've been doing it all morning. First, Corinne and I want to apologize. Last night, you were trying to talk to us, and we shut you out."

"It's okay, Sherri," Heather said. "I wasn't making much sense."

"Yes, you were," Corinne said firmly. "We just didn't listen. We just kept talking about our *own* weddings. How we were nervous and stressed like you, but that everything turned out okay. But we're not *you*, Heather. If you have doubts, let's talk about it."

"It's not too late," Sherri added. She glanced ruefully around her. "I mean, it may seem like it, but it's not. Look. If you want to break up with the guy because he wouldn't share his pickle, we're with you."

Heather couldn't help smiling. She held out her hand, palm down. "Friends forever?"

Grinning, they stacked their hands in their personal tower of power.

"Through thick and thin," they whispered.

"What's this, some new wedding-ritual-type-thing?" Adrienne's soft, mocking drawl came from behind them.

Heather held her friends' gaze. "No," she said. "It's a friendship-ritual-type-thing."

She turned. Yolanda was standing against the wall, squinting at her face in a small pocket mirror. She didn't look very happy, for a bridesmaid.

The organ music swelled into the processional march. The trumpets Ruby had insisted on blared out the notes of the classical piece she'd picked for Heather's march down the aisle.

Heather jumped at the sound.

"Are you ready?" Corinne whispered.

"Are you sure?" Sherri asked through gritted teeth.

Heather swallowed. "The only thing I'm sure of at the moment is that I'm about to pass out."

Her father appeared at her side. "That's our cue. Are we still on?"

Heather nodded. She couldn't speak.

Her father crooked his arm, and she slipped hers into it. With a last look at Heather, Sherri and Corinne took their places behind Yolanda and Adrienne. The bridesmaids slowly started down the aisle in a shimmering procession of the palest shades of yellow, green, blue, and apricot. Heather could hear the guests stir. The effect was like a pageant of soft summer colors, just as Ruby had said.

A perfect start to a perfect wedding . . .

Her father squeezed her arm. "I'm so proud of you, Heather," he murmured. "I'm proud of the woman you became."

"Because I'm perfect, right?" Heather muttered.

He turned to her, surprised. "No, Heather. Because you're so human. Imperfect, as we all are. But you always strive. And in the end, no matter how tough it is, you do the right thing."

Startled, Heather didn't have time to reply. Her feet were moving, and she was walking down the aisle. She felt a strange, numb sensation. She was dressed in a beautiful gown, walking down a white runner past a blur of faces, and she didn't feel a thing.

Reggie stood at the altar, facing her. All his earlier irritation seemed to have vanished. He looked so handsome, she noted. He smiled at her with a white flash of teeth and confidence.

Underneath the cover of her veil, Heather scanned the bride's side of the church for Jake. He should be sitting with the rest of her friends from the hospital. But she didn't see his familiar form. Where was he?

Thoughts crowded her brain. Snatches of words. Phrases. And all the while, Heather's gaze roamed over the happy faces, looking for the one face that was missing.

Reggie's house. Reggie's wedding. Reggie's club. Reggie's car. Reggie's friends.

The words buzzed in her brain. Reggie's voice, talking about *his* future. Always *my*. Always *I*. Never *ours*. And always *telling* her what she wanted, what she needed. Never *asking*. Always *assuming*.

You'll love the country club. You're so cute—within a month, you'll feel right at home here. You'll get used to not working, believe me. You love me. You love me . . .

No, Heather thought, the mists clearing from her brain at last.

I don't.

She looked at Reggie. He smiled at her complacently. *If only,* she thought distantly, *he knew what I am thinking.*

Oh, Reggie. I was flattered by your interest. I was dazzled by your looks and charm and yes, even your social standing. I was infatuated, like a schoolgirl. But I've graduated. And I realize it now—I don't love you!

The thought made her want to laugh, made her want to dance.

And why do I keep looking for Jake?

They reached the altar. Her father kissed her cheek. He stepped back to enter the pew and take his place next to her mother. The bridesmaids lined up to her left. The trumpets stopped. The church was quiet. Everyone was in place. Everyone was ready.

"Dearly Beloved," the minister began.

Heather lifted her veil and peered at him. "Uh, Reverend? Excuse me."

Reggie's head whipped around.

"I don't mean to interrupt," Heather said. "Well, actually, I do. I have something to say."

"Heather, stop it," Reggie whispered frantically. "This just isn't done."

"How do you know?" she countered. "You were late for rehearsal!"

Heather turned to face the church. "I'm terribly sorry to disappoint you, folks," she announced in a strong, clear voice. "All of you. Some of you came a long way to be here today. But this just isn't right."

The crowd began to murmur. Heather turned her back on the shocked faces and met Reggie's gaze. A mixture of fury and shock was on his face.

"I'll never forgive you for this, Heather," he hissed. "Don't come running back to me, because I won't take you back."

"I won't," she said quietly, so softly only Reggie could hear. She gently touched his sleeve, but he pulled away. Her hand dropped to her side. "Have a good life, Reggie. You'll have a happier one without me."

She turned on her toes, her beautiful white dress swirling. Her father stood a few feet behind her, looking shocked. And from the question in her mother's eyes, it was clear that Heather had some explaining to do . . . *later.* Somehow, Sherri and Corinne had moved up to flank her.

"Go girl," Corinne whispered.

Sherri poked her. "He's outside," she breathed in Heather's ear.

Heather turned, surprised. Understanding gleamed in Sherri's bright gaze, in Corinne's softer, sea-green eyes. They knew. They'd known before she had.

And in that instant, something else shone clearly in their faces. Acceptance. Love. No matter what she did. No matter who she was. No matter that she'd just left an elaborate wedding in ruins and outraged the cream of Atlanta society. Perfect or imperfect, they would be behind her. Solid and unquestioning. Friends forever.

She should have known that she could tell them any-thing. They could have helped her unravel the mysteries of her own heart.

She would tell them that. But for now, she had some-thing important to do.

Heather started toward the side door of the church. In the front pew, Ruby Tyler stood rigid, her hands like claws gripping the wood. Her face was tight with rage. For the first time, Heather saw a resemblance between her and her son. Why hadn't she seen how much Reggie looked like his mother?

As a parting gift, Heather tossed the bouquet to the woman who would no longer be her mother-in-law. Ruby had insisted on French tulips. It was only fair.

Then, in a swirl of tulle, silk organza, and extremely expensive lace, Heather ran out the door.

Twenty

 He was waiting underneath a spreading live oak tree. When he saw her, he started, but he didn't smile. His gaze was sober and watchful, as though the sight of a bride in a lavish wedding gown racing out of a packed church was completely natural.

The look made Heather's heart lift. Love expanded and filled her with so much joy it was a wonder she didn't float right toward him.

That was Jake.

Slow, careful, logical Jake.

Jake would wait until he knew for sure. He wouldn't *assume* anything about her.

But it didn't mean that he felt the same way about her. She'd been so blind. So stupid. For far too long.

Please don't let it be too late . . .

Hoisting her gown, she walked toward him across the soft grass.

"Hi," he said calmly.

"Hi," Heather answered breathlessly. "I wanted to ask you a question."

Jake nodded, waiting.

"Was I your mistake?" Heather asked. "The one you were trying to live with?"

The moment he took before he nodded almost stopped Heather's heart. Her eyes filled with tears.

"Why didn't you tell me?" she whispered.

"You were marrying Reggie. It wouldn't be fair of me. And I thought—" Jake struggled for the right words. "It was all my fault, Heather. I was too careful. Too focused on my career. I deserved to lose you."

"Well," Heather said, smiling at him through her tears, "you almost did. But you didn't. Jake, I was so stupid. It's you. It was always you."

And at that moment, Heather discovered that slow, careful Jake wasn't always so careful. He reached her in one long stride and crushed her to him.

He kissed her, a long kiss that was so passionate, so thrilling, she forgot she'd ever been kissed by anyone else before. Heather's ears rang and her knees turned liquid. Through it all, she could only hang on to Jake.

This was the love that they wrote about in books. *This* was the partnership of two people who respected and cared about each other. *This* was the passion that curled your toes and lifted your spirit.

They broke apart. "Wow," Heather breathed.

Jake gave a long, slow grin. "Yeah."

The love on his face was so dazzling that she had to duck her head and rest it against his chest. She didn't think she could hold so much happiness. She pressed close to him, feeling the reassuring beat of his heart against her ear.

His arms tightened around her. "You hear that?" he murmured. "It beats for you. The thought of not holding you like this, for the rest of my life, was killing me."

Heather tilted her head back. She looked into the face of the man she'd loved all along, and she laughed. "Jake Devereaux, you are lucky you have a friend like me in this world to save your sorry butt."

Jake's slow grin lit up every dark corner in her heart.

"Will you keep saving me, Heather?" he asked, tenderly brushing the tears from her cheeks.

"You can count on it," she told him softly. "A whole lifetime long."

She heard the rustle of silk. Sherri and Corinne were walking across the grass toward them.

"You see?" Sherri called to Jake. "We told you."

Frowning, Heather looked at him. "Told you what?"

Jake grinned. "Sherri and Corinne told me I'd better come to the wedding. When I told them I couldn't make it, they told me I was a liar. And they said I'd better show up—at least wait outside. I might be in for a surprise."

"We had a feeling you'd change your mind," Corinne told Heather with a smile.

"But you sure took your time," Sherri scolded.

Jake's arms tightened around her again. He swung her a bit in his arms. "It doesn't matter. This is the only thing that matters."

Suddenly, Sherri let loose with the ringing laugh that always made everyone around her start to smile. "Thank goodness you caved in to Ruby and got married in that big old church!" she cried.

Heather frowned. "Why? I don't get it."

"That excruciatingly lo-o-ong aisle," Sherri explained, drawing out the word. "It gave you plenty of time to change your mind." She grinned. "So if you think about it, you owe your happiness to your mother-in-law after all!"

Epilogue

Six Months Later

 Snow fell softly outside the old stone church on a quiet street in Baltimore. Inside, the pews were hung with garlands of evergreens and red velvet ribbons. Pots of white flowers stood on the small altar.

The church smelled as fresh as a pine forest. Heather breathed in the scent. It made her feel as though she was about to exchange vows in a quiet wintry glade. She liked the feeling.

But then again, everything about this wedding was perfect. For once, Heather didn't cringe at the word. At long last, it fit.

Behind her, her sister Talia was joking with Sherri and Corinne as she helped them adjust their head wraps and dresses in bright African patterns.

"You look pretty authentic, for white girls," she teased them.

"It's Heather who's going to steal the show," Corinne said. "You look so beautiful."

"I definitely think this gown suits you better than all that frou-frou stuff," Sherri agreed.

Heather smiled. "I do, too." She was wearing a simple white and gold gown of heavy silk crepe. The hem and sash were trimmed in a beaded African pattern.

Heather peeked into the small church again. Jake had already taken his place by the altar with his best friend David. His flowing white suit matched her dress.

Heather kept out of sight. She didn't want any bad luck vibes at this wedding, and she had no need to reassure herself with a last visit with the groom. These past six months had confirmed what she and Jake already knew in their hearts: they were meant to be.

At first, things had been hard. Heather had to deal with the fallout from her cancelled wedding. There were so many gifts to return, so many notes to write. There were belligerent, angry calls from Ruby. There was a last, angry scene with Reggie. It wasn't until he officially began dating Yolanda that Heather felt free to take a breath.

She'd had to cope with most of it without Jake. He'd had to leave for his residency at Johns Hopkins in Baltimore. Heather had missed him so much that her heart actually seemed to hurt. It didn't seem fair that just as she found her true love, she had to go through the days without him.

But after six weeks of job searching and struggling to pay her enormous phone bill, Heather had landed a job in Baltimore. She'd moved in with Talia until the wedding took place.

And best of all, her parents had moved, too. Her father and mother decided that since all their kids were on the East Coast, they should be, too. They'd found a condo near Talia's apartment, and the circle was complete.

At last, Heather had it all. Oh, if she'd married Reggie she would have had more money in the bank. But now she had the things that mattered. She loved her work as a patient advocate. She'd grown closer to Talia. And she and Jake managed to squeeze out as much time together as they could. Every moment was precious, filled with laughter and love.

Heather's eyes blurred as she gazed over the sea of friendly faces. Jake's mother and younger brother, his sister and her husband, her brothers, her cousins, their friends. She felt surrounded by love and family in a close, textured knit.

Her father approached her. "I wasn't sure about all this," he said, gesturing at his ceremonial dress. "Thought I'd feel ridiculous, like I was wearing a dress. But one trip to the tailor and I feel like a king. And you," he said, his eyes misting, "look like a queen."

"Thank you, Daddy," she told him as tears filled her own eyes. "And this time, I promise to go through with it."

He smiled. "This time, it's right."

"I don't know," Sherri said in an ominous tone, her green eyes dancing. "It's an awfully short aisle. Are you *ab-so-lute-ly* sure this time, Heather? You'd have to change your mind fast."

Heather grinned. "I'm sure."

"We all are," her father said. "You and Jake have a powerful love."

The music began, the soft sounds of a string quartet playing Bach. Jake's little niece Tobie took her place at the front excitedly. She wore a white dress embroidered with cowrie shells, her baby dreadlocks laced with thin white ribbons. She carried a woven basket filled with rose petals.

Behind her, Algie Stokes stood, holding a small tufted pillow with the wedding rings tied on with ribbon. Algie had recovered completely and was currently in remission. Heather and Jake had splurged and treated him and Crystal to a weekend in Baltimore so they could be there for the big day.

Sherri, Corinne, and Talia lined up after her, their heads held high. They each carried a single white orchid.

"Now *this* is a wedding!" Sherri said exultantly before stepping off on her journey down the aisle.

This time, Heather didn't feel numb as she walked down the aisle. She felt strong, full of faith and love. She felt as though she was at the still, quiet center of her life. Never had she felt more sure.

Jake waited for her, his quiet smile telling her everything she needed to know.

After their vows, the pastor would hand them an old-fashioned broom entwined with ribbons and flowers. According to tradition, if one of them stumbled as they jumped over it, the other would be the boss of the house. Heather had a feeling they would both sail over it easily.

Because this was real love. Equal partners. Love in one hand, laughter in the other. The two of them looking ahead to a future together, their faces in the same direction.

She took her place beside Jake. He slipped his hand into hers. They exchanged a brief, private glance before turning to face the reverend.

Now this, Heather thought, *will be a life.*

Avon Flare Presents
Award-winning Author
JEAN THESMAN

MOLLY DONNELLY   72252-6/ $4.50 US/ $6.50 Can

On December 7, 1941, the Japanese bombed Pearl Harbor, and the world changed forever. It was the beginning of World War II and for Molly Donnelly, it was the end of childhood. But it was also a time of great discoveries—about first dates, first kisses, falling in love, and about all the wonderful possibilities that lay ahead when the war was over.

RACHEL CHANCE   71378-0/ $3.50 US/ $4.25 Can

THE RAIN CATCHERS

71711-5/ $4.50 US/ $5.99 Can

THE WHITNEY COUSINS: HEATHER

75869-5/ $2.95 US/ $3.50 Can

CATTAIL MOON   72504-5/ $4.50 US/ $5.99 Can